In Ghostly Japan

Lafcadio Hearn (1850–1904), born in Greece to an Anglo-Irish father and a Greek mother, was brought up in Greece and Ireland. He moved to the US when he was nineteen, and then to Japan in 1890, where he spent the rest of his life teaching and writing. Hearn was one of the first great interpreters of things Japanese for Western readers. His long residence in Japan, combined with his perfect insight and sympathy, keen intellect, poetic imagination, and clear writing style have ensured him a devoted readership among both foreigners and Japanese for over a century.

THE MOUNTAIN OF SKULLS

In Ghostly Japan

by Lafcadio Hearn

霊

の

日

本

TUTTLE PUBLISHING
Boston • Rutland, Vermont • Tokyo

Published by Tuttle Publishing, an imprint of Periplus Editions (HK) Ltd.

First Tuttle edition, 1971
LCC Card No. 79-138068

ISBN 0-8048-3361-2
ISBN 4-8053-0749-8 (for sale in Japan only)

Distributed by

Japan
Tuttle Publishing
Yaekari Building, 3rd Floor
5-4-12 Osaki, Shinagawa-ku
Tokyo 141-0032
Tel: (03) 5437 0171; Fax: (03) 5437 0755
Email: tuttle-sales@gol.com

North America, Latin America & Europe
Tuttle Publishing
364 Innovation Drive
North Clarendon, VT 05759-9436
Tel: (802) 773 8930; Fax: (802) 773 6993
Email: info@tuttlepublishing.com
www.tuttlepublishing.com

Asia Pacific
Berkeley Books Pte. Ltd.
130 Joo Seng Road, #06-01/03
Singapore 368357
Tel: (65) 6280 1330; Fax: (65) 6280 6290
Email: inquiries@periplus.com.sg
www.periplus.com

04 06 08 09 07 05
1 3 5 7 8 6 4 2

Printed in Singapore

Table of Contents

List of Illustrations

Full Page

Illustrations in the Text

Publisher's Foreword

❧

LAFCADIO HEARN is almost as Japanese as haiku. Both are an art form, an institution in Japan. Haiku is indigenous to the nation; Hearn became a Japanese citizen and married a Japanese, taking the name Yakumo Koizumi. His flight from Western materialism brought him to Japan in 1890. His search for beauty and tranquility, for pleasing customs and lasting values, kept him there the rest of his life, a confirmed Japanophile. He became the great interpreter of things Japanese to the West. His keen intellect, poetic imagination and wonderfully clear style permitted him to penetrate to the very essence of things Japanese.

In his *In Ghostly Japan*, Hearn conjures up deathless images of ghouls and goblins, interwoven with the folklore, superstitions, and traditions of the nation. These in turn have their roots in early ancestor worship—"the root of all reli-

gions." These stories are not all ghostly or
ghastly either. "Bits of Poetry" is a delightful
digression into verse, and "Japanese Buddhist
Proverbs" are in the spirit of the idealization.

In Ghostly Japan

IN GHOSTLY JAPAN

Yoru bakari
Miru mono nari to
Omou-nayo !
Hiru saë yumé no
Ukiyo nari-kéri.

Think not that dreams appear to the dreamer
only at night : the dream of this world of pain
appears to us even by day.

In Ghostly Japan

Fragment

. . . .

AND it was at the hour of sunset that they came to the foot of the mountain. There was in that place no sign of life, — neither token of water, nor trace of plant, nor shadow of flying bird, — nothing but desolation rising to desolation. And the summit was lost in heaven.

Then the Bodhisattva said to his young companion : — "What you have asked to see will be shown to you. But the place of the Vision is far ; and the way is rude. Follow after me, and do not fear : strength will be given you."

Twilight gloomed about them as they climbed. There was no beaten path, nor any mark of former human visitation ; and the way was over an endless heaping of tumbled fragments that rolled or turned beneath the foot. Sometimes a mass dislodged would clatter down with hollow echoings; — sometimes the substance trodden would burst like an empty shell. . . . Stars pointed and thrilled; — and the darkness deepened.

" Do not fear, my son," said the Bodhisattva, guiding : " danger there is none, though the way be grim."

Under the stars they climbed, — fast, fast, — mounting by help of power superhuman. High zones of mist they passed ; and they saw below them, ever widening as they climbed, a soundless flood of cloud, like the tide of a milky sea.

Hour after hour they climbed ; — and forms invisible yielded to their tread with dull soft crashings ; — and faint cold fires lighted and died at every breaking.

And once the pilgrim-youth laid hand on a something smooth that was not stone, — and lifted it, — and dimly saw the cheekless gibe of death.

" Linger not thus, my son !" urged the voice of the teacher ; — " the summit that we must gain is very far away !"

On through the dark they climbed, — and felt continually beneath them the soft strange break-ings, — and saw the icy fires worm and die, — till the rim of the night turned grey, and the stars began to fail, and the east began to bloom.

Yet still they climbed, — fast, fast, — mounting by help of power superhuman. About them now was frigidness of death, — and silence tremendous. . . . A gold flame kindled in the east.

Then first to the pilgrim's gaze the steeps revealed their nakedness ; — and a trembling seized him, — and a ghastly fear. For there was not any ground, — neither beneath him nor about him nor above him, — but a heaping only, monstrous and measureless, of skulls and fragments of skulls and dust of bone, — with a shimmer of shed teeth strown through the drift of it, like the shimmer of scrags of shell in the wrack of a tide.

" Do not fear, my son ! " cried the voice of the Bodhisattva ; — " only the strong of heart can win to the place of the Vision ! "

Behind them the world had vanished. Nothing remained but the clouds beneath, and the sky above, and the heaping of skulls between, — up-slanting out of sight.

Then the sun climbed with the climbers ; and there was no warmth in the light of him, but coldness sharp as a sword. And the horror of stupendous height, and the nightmare of stupendous depth, and the terror of silence, ever grew and grew, and weighed upon the pilgrim, and held his feet, — so that suddenly all power departed from him, and he moaned like a sleeper in dreams.

" Hasten, hasten, my son! " cried the Bodhisattva : "the day is brief, and the summit is very far away."

But the pilgrim shrieked, —

" I fear! I fear unspeakably! — and the power has departed from me! "

" The power will return, my son," made answer the Bodhisattva. . . . " Look now below you and above you and about you, and tell me what you see."

" I cannot," cried the pilgrim, trembling and clinging ; — " I dare not look beneath! Before me and about me there is nothing but skulls of men."

" And yet, my son," said the Bodhisattva, laughing softly, — " and yet you do not know of what this mountain is made."

The other, shuddering, repeated : —

" I fear! — unutterably I fear! . . . there is nothing but skulls of men! "

"A mountain of skulls it is," responded the Bodhisattva. "But know, my son, that all of them ARE YOUR OWN! Each has at some time been the nest of your dreams and delusions and desires. Not even one of them is the skull of any other being. All, — all without exception, — have been yours, in the billions of your former lives."

. . . .

Furisodé

Furisodé

RECENTLY, while passing through a little street tenanted chiefly by dealers in old wares, I noticed a *furisodé*, or long-sleeved robe, of the rich purple tint called *murasaki*, hanging before one of the shops. It was a robe such as might have been worn by a lady of rank in the time of the Tokugawa. I stopped to look at the five crests upon it; and in the same moment there came to my recollection this legend of a similar robe said to have once caused the destruction of Yedo.

Nearly two hundred and fifty years ago, the daughter of a rich merchant of the city of the Shōguns, while attending some temple-festival, perceived in the crowd a young samurai of remarkable beauty, and immediately fell in love with him. Unhappily for her, he disappeared in the press before she could learn through her attendants who he was or whence he had come.

But his image remained vivid in her memory, — even to the least detail of his costume. The holiday attire then worn by samurai youths was scarcely less brilliant than that of young girls; and the upper dress of this handsome stranger had seemed wonderfully beautiful to the enamoured maiden. She fancied that by wearing a robe of like quality and color, bearing the same crest, she might be able to attract his notice on some future occasion.

Accordingly she had such a robe made, with very long sleeves, according to the fashion of the period; and she prized it greatly. She wore it whenever she went out; and when at home she would suspend it in her room, and try to imagine the form of her unknown beloved within it. Sometimes she would pass hours before it, — dreaming and weeping by turns. And she would pray to the gods and the Buddhas that she might win the young man's affection, — often repeating the invocation of the Nichiren sect: *Namu myō hō rengé kyō !*

But she never saw the youth again; and she pined with longing for him, and sickened, and died, and was buried. After her burial, the long-sleeved robe that she had so much prized was given to the Buddhist temple of which her family were parishioners. It is an old custom to thus dispose of the garments of the dead.

The priest was able to sell the robe at a good price; for it was a costly silk, and bore no trace of the tears that had fallen upon it. It was bought by a girl of about the same age as the dead lady. She wore it only one day. Then she fell sick, and began to act strangely, — crying out that she was haunted by the vision of a beautiful young man, and that for love of him she was going to die. And within a little while she died ; and the long-sleeved robe was a second time presented to the temple.

Again the priest sold it; and again it became the property of a young girl, who wore it only once. Then she also sickened, and talked of a beautiful shadow, and died, and was buried. And the robe was given a third time to the temple ; and the priest wondered and doubted.

Nevertheless he ventured to sell the luckless garment once more. Once more it was pur-chased by a girl and once more worn ; and the wearer pined and died. And the robe was given a fourth time to the temple.

Then the priest felt sure that there was some

evil influence at work; and he told his acolytes to make a fire in the temple-court, and to burn the robe.

So they made a fire, into which the robe was thrown. But as the silk began to burn, there suddenly appeared upon it dazzling characters of flame, — the characters of the invocation, *Namu myō hō rengé kyō;* — and these, one by one, leaped like great sparks to the temple roof; and the temple took fire.

Embers from the burning temple presently dropped upon neighbouring roofs; and the whole street was soon ablaze. Then a sea-wind, rising, blew destruction into further streets; and the conflagration spread from street to street, and from district into district, till nearly the whole of the city was consumed. And this calamity, which occurred upon the eighteenth day of the first month of the first year of Meiréki (1655), is still remembered in Tōkyō as the *Furisodé-Kwaji*, — the Great Fire of the Long-sleeved Robe.

According to a story-book called *Kibun-Daijin*, the name of the girl who caused the robe to be made was O-Samé; and she was the daughter of Hikoyémon, a wine-merchant of Hyakushō-machi, in the district of Azabu. Because of her beauty she was also called Azabu-Komachi, or the Komachi of Azabu.[1] The same book says that the temple of the tradition was a Nichiren temple called Hon-myōji, in the district of Hongo; and that the crest upon the robe was a *kikyō*-flower. But there are many different versions of the story; and I distrust the *Kibun-Daijin* because it asserts that the beautiful samurai was not really a man, but a transformed dragon, or water-serpent, that used to inhabit the lake at Uyéno, — *Shinobazu-no-Iké*.

---

[1] After more than a thousand years, the name of Komachi, or Ono-no-Komachi, is still celebrated in Japan. She was the most beautiful woman of her time, and so great a poet that she could move heaven by her verses, and cause rain to fall in time of drought. Many men loved her in vain; and many are said to have died for love of her. But misfortunes visited her when her youth had passed; and, after having been reduced to the uttermost want, she became a beggar, and died at last upon the public highway, near Kyōto. As it was thought shameful to bury her in the foul rags found upon her, some poor person gave a worn-out summer-robe (*katabira*) to wrap her body in; and she was interred near Arashiyama at a spot still pointed out to travellers as the "Place of the Katabira" (*Katabira-no-Tsuchi*).

Incense

Incense

I

I SEE, rising out of darkness, a lotos in a vase. Most of the vase is invisible; but I know that it is of bronze, and that its glimpsing handles are bodies of dragons. Only the lotos is fully illuminated: three pure white flowers, and five great leaves of gold and green, — gold above, green on the upcurling under-surface, — an artificial lotos. It is bathed by a slanting stream of sunshine; — the darkness beneath and beyond is the dusk of a temple-chamber. I do not see the opening through which the radiance pours; but I am aware that it is a small window shaped in the outline-form of a temple-bell.

The reason that I see the lotos — one memory of my first visit to a Buddhist sanctuary — is that there has come to me an odor of incense. Often when I smell incense, this vision defines; and usually thereafter other sensations of my first day in Japan revive in swift succession with almost painful acuteness.

It is almost ubiquitous, — this perfume of incense. It makes one element of the faint but complex and never-to-be-forgotten odor of the Far East. It haunts the dwelling-house not less than the temple, — the home of the peasant not less than the yashiki of the prince. Shintō shrines, indeed, are free from it ; — incense being an abomination to the elder gods. But wherever Buddhism lives there is incense. In every house containing a Buddhist shrine or Buddhist tablets, incense is burned at certain times ; and in even the rudest country solitudes you will find incense smouldering before wayside images, — little stone figures of Fudō, Jizō, or Kwannon. Many experiences of travel, — strange impressions of sound as well as of sight, — remain associated in my own memory with that fragrance : — vast silent shadowed avenues leading to weird old shrines ; — mossed flights of worn steps ascending to temples that moulder above the clouds ; — joyous tumult of festival nights ; — sheeted funeral-trains gliding by in glimmer of lanterns ; — murmur of household prayer in fishermen's huts on far wild coasts; — and visions of desolate little graves marked only by threads of blue smoke ascending, — graves of pet animals or birds remembered by simple hearts in the hour of prayer to Amida, the Lord of Immeasurable Light.

But the odor of which I speak is that of cheap incense only, — the incense in general use. There are many other kinds of incense; and the range of quality is amazing. A bundle of common incense-rods — (they are about as thick as an ordinary pencil-lead, and somewhat longer) — can be bought for a few sen; while a bundle of better quality, presenting to inexperienced eyes only some difference in color, may cost several yen, and be cheap at the price. Still costlier sorts of incense, — veritable luxuries, — take the form of lozenges, wafers, pastilles; and a small envelope of such material may be worth four or five pounds–sterling. But the commercial and industrial questions relating to Japanese incense represent the least interesting part of a remarkably curious subject.

II

Curious indeed, but enormous by reason of its infinity of tradition and detail. I am afraid even to think of the size of the volume that would be needed to cover it. . . . Such a work would properly begin with some brief account of the earliest knowledge and use of aromatics in Japan. It would next treat of the records and legends of the first introduction of Buddhist incense from Korea, — when King Shōmyō of Kudara, in 551 A. D., sent to the island-empire a collection of sutras, an image of the Buddha, and one complete set of furniture for a temple. Then something would have to be said about those classifications of incense which were made during the tenth century, in the periods of Engi and of Tenryaku, — and about the report of the ancient state-councillor, Kimitaka-Sangi, who visited China in the latter part of the thirteenth century, and transmitted to the Emperor Yōmei the wisdom of the Chinese concerning incense. Then mention should be made of the ancient incenses still preserved in various Japanese temples, and of the famous fragments of *ranjatai* (publicly exhibited at

Nara in the tenth year of Meiji) which furnished supplies to the three great captains, Nobunaga, Hideyoshi, and Iyeyasu. After this should follow an outline of the history of mixed incenses made in Japan, — with notes on the classifications devised by the luxurious Takauji, and on the nomenclature established later by Ashikaga Yoshimasa, who collected one hundred and thirty varieties of incense, and invented for the more precious of them names recognized even to this day, — such as " Blossom-Showering," " Smoke-of-Fuji," and " Flower-of-the-Pure-Law." Examples ought to be given likewise of traditions attaching to historical incenses preserved in several princely families ; together with specimens of those hereditary recipes for incense-making which have been transmitted from generation to generation through hundreds of years, and are still called after their august inventors, — as " the Method of Hina-Dainagon," " the Method of Sentō-In," etc. Recipes also should be given of those strange incenses made *" to imitate the perfume of the lotos, the smell of the summer breeze, and the odor of the autumn wind."* Some legends of the great period of incense-luxury should be cited, — such as the story of

Sué Owari-no-Kami, who built for himself a palace of incense-woods, and set fire to it on the night of his revolt, when the smoke of its burning perfumed the land to a distance of twelve miles. . . . Of course the mere compilation of materials for a history of mixed-incenses would entail the study of a host of documents, treatises, and books, — particularly of such strange works as the *Kun-Shū-Rui-Shō*, or " Incense-Collector's-Classifying-Manual " ; — containing the teachings of the Ten Schools of the Art of Mixing Incense ; directions as to the best seasons for incense-making ; and instructions about the " *different kinds of fire* " to be used for burning incense — (one kind is called " literary fire," and another " military fire ") ; together with rules for pressing the ashes of a censer into various artistic designs corresponding to season and occasion. . . . A special chapter should certainly be given to the incense-bags (*kusadama*) hung up in houses to drive away goblins, — and to the smaller incense-bags formerly carried about the person as a protection against evil spirits. Then a very large part of the work would have to be devoted to the religious uses and legends of incense, — a huge subject in itself. There would also have to be considered the curious history of the old " incense-assemblies," whose elaborate ceremonial could be explained only by help of numerous diagrams. One chapter at least would be required for the subject of the ancient importation of incense-materials from India, China, Annam, Siam, Cambodia, Ceylon, Sumatra, Java, Borneo, and various islands of the Malay archipelago, — places all named in rare books about incense. And a final chapter should treat of the romantic literature of incense, — the poems, stories, and dramas in which incense-rites are mentioned; and especially those love-songs comparing the body to incense, and passion to the eating flame : —

Even as burns the perfume lending my robe its fragrance,
Smoulders my life away, consumed by the pain of longing!

. . . The merest outline of the subject is terrifying ! I shall attempt nothing more than a few notes about the religious, the luxurious, and the ghostly uses of incense.

III

The common incense everywhere burned by poor people before Buddhist icons is called *an-soku-kō*. This is very cheap. Great quantities of it are burned by pilgrims in the bronze censers set before the entrances of famous temples; and in front of roadside images you may often see bundles of it. These are for the use of pious wayfarers, who pause before every Buddhist image on their path to repeat a brief prayer and, when possible, to set a few rods smouldering at the feet of the statue. But in rich temples, and during great religious ceremonies, much more expensive incense is used. Altogether three classes of perfumes are employed in Buddhist rites : *kō*, or incense-proper, in many varieties — (the word literally means only " fragrant substance ") ; — *dzukō*, an odorous ointment ; and *makkō*, a fragrant powder. *Kō* is burned ; *dzukō* is rubbed upon the hands of the priest as an ointment of purification ; and *makkō* is sprinkled about the sanctuary. This *makkō* is said to be identical with the sandalwood-powder so frequently mentioned in Buddhist texts. But it is only the true incense which can be said to bear an important relation to the religious service.

" Incense," declares the *Soshi-Ryaku*,[1] " is the Messenger of Earnest Desire. When the rich Sudatta wished to invite the Buddha to a repast, he made use of incense. He was wont to ascend to the roof of his house on the eve of the day of the entertainment, and to remain standing there all night, holding a censer of precious incense. And as often as he did thus, the Buddha never failed to come on the following day at the exact time desired."

This text plainly implies that incense, as a burnt-offering, symbolizes the pious desires of the faithful. But it symbolizes other things also ; and it has furnished many remarkable similes to Buddhist literature. Some of these, and not the least interesting, occur in prayers, of which the following, from the book called *Hōji-san*[2] is a striking example : —

— " *Let my body remain pure like a censer !* — *let my thought be ever as a fire of wisdom, purely consuming the incense of sîla and of dhyâna*,[3] —

[1] " Short [or Epitomized] History of Priests."
[2] " The Praise of Pious Observances."
[3] By *sîla* is meant the observance of the rules of purity

that so may I do homage to all the Buddhas in the Ten Directions of the Past, the Present, and the Future!"

Sometimes in Buddhist sermons the destruction of Karma by virtuous effort is likened to the burning of incense by a pure flame, — sometimes, again, the life of man is compared to the smoke of incense. In his " Hundred Writings "(*Hyaku-tsū-kiri-kami*), the Shinshū priest Myōden says, quoting from the Buddhist work *Kujikkajō*, or " Ninety Articles " : —

" In the burning of incense we see that so long as any incense remains, so long does the burning continue, and the smoke mount skyward. Now the breath of this body of ours, — this imperma- nent combination of Earth, Water, Air, and Fire, — is like that smoke. And the changing of the incense into cold ashes when the flame expires is an emblem of the changing of our bodies into ashes when our funeral pyres have burnt them- selves out."

He also tells us about that Incense-Paradise of which every believer ought to be reminded by the

in act and thought. *Dhyâna* (called by Japanese Buddhists *Zenjō*) is one of the higher forms of meditation.

perfume of earthly incense: — " In the Thirty-Second Vow for the Attainment of the Paradise of Wondrous Incense," he says, " it is written: — ' *That Paradise is formed of hundreds of thousands of different kinds of incense, and of substances incalculably precious ; — the beauty of it incomparably exceeds anything in the heavens or in the sphere of man ; — the fragrance of it perfumes all the worlds of the Ten Directions of Space ; and all who perceive that odor practise Buddha-deeds.'* In ancient times there were men of superior wisdom and virtue who, by reason of their vow, obtained perception of the odor; but we, who are born with inferior wisdom and virtue in these later days, cannot obtain such perception. Nevertheless it will be well for us, when we smell the incense kindled before the image of Amida, to imagine that its odor is the wonderful fragrance of Paradise, and to repeat the *Nembutsu* in gratitude for the mercy of the Buddha."

IV

But the use of incense in Japan is not confined to religious rites and ceremonies: indeed the costlier kinds of incense are manufactured chiefly for social entertainments. Incense-burning has been an amusement of the aristocracy ever since the thirteenth century. Probably you have heard of the Japanese tea-ceremonies, and their curious Buddhist history; and I suppose that every foreign collector of Japanese *bric-à-brac* knows something about the luxury to which these ceremonies at one period attained, — a luxury well attested by the quality of the beautiful utensils formerly employed in them. But there were, and still are, incense-ceremonies much more elaborate and costly than the tea-ceremonies, — and also much more interesting. Besides music, embroidery, poetical composition and other branches of the old-fashioned female education, the young lady of pre-Meiji days was expected to acquire three especially polite accomplishments, — the art of arranging flowers, (*ikébana*), the art of ceremonial tea-making (*cha-no-yu* or *cha-no-é*),[1] and the etiquette of incense-parties (*kō-kwai* or *kō-é*). Incense-parties were invented before the time of the Ashikaga shōguns, and were most in vogue during the peaceful period of the Tokugawa rule. With the fall of the shōgunate they went out of fashion; but recently they have been to some extent revived. It is not likely, however, that they will again become really fashionable in the old sense, — partly because they represented rare forms of social refinement that never can be revived, and partly because of their costliness.

In translating *kō-kwai* as "incense-party," I use the word "party" in the meaning that it takes in such compounds as "card-party," "whist-party," "chess-party"; — for a *kō-kwai* is a meeting held only with the object of playing a game, — a very curious game. There are several kinds of incense-games; but in all of them

---

[1] Girls are still trained in the art of arranging flowers, and in the etiquette of the dainty, though somewhat tedious, *cha-no-yu*. Buddhist priests have long enjoyed a reputation as teachers of the latter. When the pupil has reached a certain degree of proficiency, she is given a diploma or certificate. The tea used in these ceremonies is a powdered tea of remarkable fragrance, — the best qualities of which fetch very high prices.

the contest depends upon the ability to remember and to name different kinds of incense by the perfume alone. That variety of *kō-kwai* called *Jitchū-kō* ("ten-burning-incense") is generally conceded to be the most amusing; and I shall try to tell you how it is played.

The numeral "ten," in the Japanese, or rather Chinese name of this diversion, does not refer to ten kinds, but only to ten packages of incense; for *Jitchū-kō*, besides being the most amusing, is the very simplest of incense-games, and is played with only four kinds of incense. One kind must be supplied by the guests invited to the party; and three are furnished by the person who gives the entertainment. Each of the latter three supplies of incense — usually prepared in packages containing one hundred wafers — is divided into four parts; and each part is put into a separate paper numbered or marked so as to indicate the quality. Thus four packages are prepared of the incense classed as No. 1, four of incense No. 2, and four of incense No. 3, — or twelve in all. But the incense given by the guests, — always called "guest-incense" — is not divided: it is only put into a wrapper marked with an abbrevi-

ation of the Chinese character signifying " guest."
Accordingly we have a total of thirteen packages
to start with; but three are to be used in the
preliminary sampling, or " experimenting " — as
the Japanese term it, — after the following
manner.

We shall suppose the game to be arranged for
a party of six, — though there is no rule limiting
the number of players. The six take their places
in line, or in a half-circle — if the room be small;
but they do not sit close together, for reasons
which will presently appear. Then the host, or
the person appointed to act as incense-burner,
prepares a package of the incense classed as
No. 1, kindles it in a censer, and passes the
censer to the guest occupying the first seat[1], with
the announcement : — "This is incense No. 1."
The guest receives the censer according to the
graceful etiquette required in the *kō-kwai*, inhales
the perfume, and passes on the vessel to his
neighbor, who receives it in like manner and
passes it to the third guest, who presents it to

[1] The places occupied by guests in a Japanese *zashiki*,
or reception-room, are numbered from the alcove of the
apartment. The place of the most honored is immediately
before the alcove: this is the first seat; and the rest are
numbered from it, usually to the left.

the fourth, — and so on. When the censer has gone the round of the party, it is returned to the incense-burner. One package of incense No. 2, and one of No. 3, are similarly prepared, announced, and tested. But with the "guest-incense" no experiment is made. The player should be able to remember the different odors of the incenses tested; and he is expected to identify the guest-incense at the proper time merely by the unfamiliar quality of its fragrance.

The original thirteen packages having thus by "experimenting" been reduced to ten, each player is given one set of ten small tablets — usually of gold-lacquer, — every set being differently ornamented. The backs only of these tablets are decorated; and the decoration is nearly always a floral design of some sort: — thus one set might be decorated with chrysanthemums in gold, another with tufts of iris-plants, another with a spray of plum-blossoms, etc. But the faces of the tablets bear numbers or marks; and each set comprises three tablets numbered "1," three numbered "2," three numbered "3," and one marked with the character signifying "guest." After these tablet-sets have been distributed, a box called the "tablet-box" is placed before the first player; and all is ready for the real game.

The incense-burner retires behind a little screen, shuffles the flat packages like so many cards, takes the uppermost, prepares its contents in the censer, and then, returning to the party, sends the censer upon its round. This time, of course, he does not announce what kind of incense he has used. As the censer passes from hand to hand, each player, after inhaling the fume, puts into the tablet-box one tablet bearing that mark or number which he supposes to be the mark or number of the incense he has smelled. If, for example, he thinks the incense to be "guest-incense," he drops into the box that one of his tablets marked with the ideograph meaning "guest;" or if he believes that he has inhaled the perfume of No. 2, he puts into the box a tablet numbered "2." When the round is over, tablet-box and censer are both returned to the incense-burner. He takes the six tablets out of the box, and wraps them up in the paper which contained the incense guessed about. The tablets themselves keep the personal as well as the general record, — since each player remembers the particular design upon his own set.

The remaining nine packages of incense are consumed and judged in the same way, according to the chance order in which the shuffling has placed them.   When all the incense has been used, the tablets are taken out of their wrappings, the record is officially put into writing, and the victor of the day is announced.   I here offer the translation of such a record : it will serve to explain, almost at a glance, all the complications of the game.

According to this record the player who used the tablets decorated with the design called " Young Pine," made but two mistakes ; while the holder of the " White-Lily " set made only one correct guess.   But it is quite a feat to make ten correct judgments in succession.   The olfactory nerves are apt to become somewhat numbed long before the game is concluded ; and therefore it is customary during the *Kō-kwai* to rinse the mouth at intervals with pure vinegar, by which operation the sensitivity is partially restored.

To the Japanese original of the foregoing record were appended the names of the players, the date of the entertainment, and the name of the place where the party was held.   It is the

RECORD OF A KŌ-KWAI.

Names given to the six sets of tablets used, according to the decorative designs on the back:—

Order in which the ten packages of incense were used:—

Guesses recorded by the numbers on the tablet; correct guesses being marked *:—

	1	2	3	4	5	6	7	8	9	10	Number of correct guesses:—
	No. III.	No. I.	— "Guest"	No. II.	No. I.	No. III.	No. II.	No. I.	No. III.	No. II.	
"Gold Chrysanthemum"	1	3	1	2*	"Guest"	1	2*	2	3*	3	3.
"Young Bamboo"	3*	1*	2	2*	1*	"Guest"	3	2	1	3	4.
"Red Peony"	"Guest"	1*	1	2*	3	1	3	2	3*	1	3.
"White Lily"	1	3	2	3	2	2	3	3	"Guest"	2*	1.
"Young Pine"	3*	1*	"Guest"*	3	1*	2	2*	1*	3*	2*	8. (Winner.)
"Cherry-Blossom-in-a-Mist"	1	3	"Guest"*	2*	1*	3*	1	2	3*	2*	6.

NAMES OF INCENSE USED.

I. . . . . "Tasogare" ("Who-is-there?"—i. e., "Evening-Dusk").

II. . . . . "Baikwa" ("Plum flower").

III. . . . . "Wakakusa" ("Young Grass").

IV. . . . ("Guest Incense") . . "Yamaji-no-Tsuyu" ("Dew-on-the-Mountain-Path").

custom in some families to enter all such records in a book especially made for the purpose, and furnished with an index which enables the *Kō-kwai* player to refer immediately to any interesting fact belonging to the history of any past game.

The reader will have noticed that the four kinds of incense used were designated by very pretty names. The incense first mentioned, for example, is called by the poets' name for the gloaming, — *Tasogaré* (lit. : " Who is there ? " or " Who is it ? ") — a word which in this relation hints of the toilet-perfume that reveals some charming presence to the lover waiting in the dusk. Perhaps some curiosity will be felt regarding the composition of these incenses. I can give the Japanese recipes for two sorts ; but I have not been able to identify all of the materials named : —

Recipe for Yamaji-no-Tsuyu.

Ingredients.	Proportions.	
	about	
Jinkō (aloes-wood)	4 *mommé* (½ oz.)	
Chōji (cloves)	4 " "	
Kunroku (olibanum)	4 " "	To 21 pastilles.
Hakkō (artemisia Schmidtiana) . .	4 " "	
Jakō (musk)	1 *bu* (⅛ oz.)	
Kōkō (?)	4 *mommé* (½ oz.)	

Recipe for Baikwa.

Ingredients.	Proportions.	
		about
Jinkō (aloes)	20 *mommé*	(2½ oz.)
Chōji (cloves)	12 "	(1½ oz.)
Kōkō (?)	8⅓ "	(1 1/40 oz.)
Byakudan (sandal-wood)	4 "	(½ oz.)
Kanshō (spikenard)	2 *bu*	(¼ oz.)
Kwakkō (Bishop's-wort?)	1 *bu* 2 *shu*	(8/16 oz.)
Kunroku (olibanum)	3 " 3 "	(15/22 oz.)
Shōmokkō (?)	2 "	(¼ oz.)
Jakō (musk)	3 " 2 *shu*	(7/16 oz.)
Ryūnō (refined Borneo Camphor)	3 *shu*	(⅜ oz.)

To 50 pastilles.

The incense used at a *Kō-kwai* ranges in value, according to the style of the entertainment, from $2.50 to $30.00 per envelope of 100 wafers — wafers usually not more than one-fourth of an inch in diameter. Sometimes an incense is used worth even more than $30.00 per envelope : this contains *ranjatai*, an aromatic of which the perfume is compared to that of " musk mingled with orchid-flowers." But there is some incense, — never sold, — which is much more precious than *ranjatai*, — incense valued less for its composition than for its history : I mean the incense brought centuries ago from China or from India by the Buddhist missionaries, and presented to princes or to other persons of high rank. Several ancient Japanese temples also include such foreign incense among their treasures. And very rarely a little of this priceless material is contributed to an incense-party, — much as in Europe, on very extraordinary occasions, some banquet is glorified by the production of a wine several hundred years old.

Like the tea-ceremonies, the *Kō-kwai* exact observance of a very complex and ancient etiquette. But this subject could interest few readers; and I shall only mention some of the rules regarding preparations and precautions. First of all, it is required that the person invited to an incense-party shall attend the same in as *odorless* a condition as possible : a lady, for instance, must not use hair-oil, or put on any dress that has been kept in a perfumed chest-of-drawers. Furthermore, the guest should prepare for the contest by taking a prolonged hot bath, and should eat only the lightest and least odorous kind of food before going to the rendezvous. It is forbidden to leave the room during the game, or to open any door or window, or to indulge in needless conversation. Finally I may observe that, while judging the incense, a player is expected to take not less than three inhalations, or more than five.

In this economical era, the *Kō-kwai* takes of necessity a much humbler form than it assumed in the time of the great daimyō, of the princely abbots, and of the military aristocracy. A full set of the utensils required for the game can now be had for about $50.00; but the materials are of the poorest kind. The old-fashioned sets were fantastically expensive. Some were worth thousands of dollars. The incense-burner's desk, — the writing-box, paper-box, tablet-box, etc., — the various stands or *dai*, — were of the costliest gold-lacquer; — the pincers and other instruments were of gold, curiously worked; — and the censer — whether of precious metal, bronze, or porcelain, — was always a *chef-d'œuvre*, designed by some artist of renown.

V

Although the original signification of incense in Buddhist ceremonies was chiefly symbolical, there is good reason to suppose that various beliefs older than Buddhism, — some, perhaps, peculiar to the race; others probably of Chinese or Korean derivation, — began at an early period to influence the popular use of incense in Japan. Incense is still burned in the presence of a corpse with the idea that its fragrance shields both corpse and newly-parted soul from malevolent demons; and by the peasants it is often burned also to drive away goblins and the evil powers presiding over diseases. But formerly it was used to summon spirits as well as to banish them. Allusions to its employment in various weird rites may be found in some of the old dramas and romances. One particular sort of incense, imported from China, was said to have the power of calling up human spirits. This was the wizard-incense referred to in such ancient love-songs as the following : —

> " *I have heard of the magical incense that summons the souls*
> *of the absent :*
> *Would I had some to burn, in the nights when I wait*
> *alone !* "

There is an interesting mention of this incense in the Chinese book, *Shang-hai-king*. It was called *Fwan-hwan-hiang* (by Japanese pronunciation, *Hangon-kō*), or " Spirit-Recalling-Incense ; " and it was made in Tso-Chau, or the District of the Ancestors, situated by the Eastern Sea. To summon the ghost of any dead person — or

THE MAGICAL INCENSE

even that of a living person, according to some authorities, — it was only necessary to kindle some of the incense, and to pronounce certain words, while keeping the mind fixed upon the memory of that person. Then, in the smoke of the incense, the remembered face and form would appear.

In many old Japanese and Chinese books mention is made of a famous story about this incense, — a story of the Chinese Emperor Wu, of the Han dynasty. When the Emperor had lost his beautiful favorite, the Lady Li, he sorrowed so much that fears were entertained for his reason. But all efforts made to divert his mind from the thought of her proved unavailing. One day he ordered some Spirit-Recalling-Incense to be procured, that he might summon her from the dead. His counsellors prayed him to forego his purpose, declaring that the vision could only intensify his grief. But he gave no heed to their advice, and himself performed the rite, — kindling the incense, and keeping his mind fixed upon the memory of the Lady Li. Presently, within the thick blue smoke arising from the incense, the outline of a feminine form became visible. It defined, took tints of life, slowly became luminous; and the Emperor recognized the form of his beloved. At first the apparition was faint; but it soon became distinct as a living person, and seemed with each moment to grow more beautiful. The Emperor whispered to the vision, but received no answer. He called aloud, and the presence made no sign. Then unable to control himself, he approached the censer. But the instant that he touched the smoke, the phantom trembled and vanished.

Japanese artists are still occasionally inspired by the legends of the *Hangon-kō*. Only last year, in Tōkyō, at an exhibition of new kake-mono, I saw a picture of a young wife kneeling before an alcove wherein the smoke of the magical incense was shaping the shadow of the absent husband.[1]

Although the power of making visible the forms of the dead has been claimed for one sort

[1] Among the curious Tōkyō inventions of 1898 was a new variety of cigarettes called *Hangon-sō*, or "Herb of Hangon," — a name suggesting that their smoke operated like the spirit-summoning incense. As a matter of fact, the chemical action of the tobacco-smoke would define, upon a paper fitted into the mouth-piece of each cigarette, the photographic image of a dancing-girl.

of incense only, the burning of any kind of incense is supposed to summon viewless spirits in
multitude. These come to devour the smoke.
They are called *Jiki-kō-ki*, or "incense-eating
goblins;" and they belong to the fourteenth of
the thirty-six classes of Gaki (*prêtas*) recognized
by Japanese Buddhism. They are the ghosts of
men who anciently, for the sake of gain, made
or sold bad incense; and by the evil karma of
that action they now find themselves in the state
of hunger-suffering spirits, and compelled to seek
their only food in the smoke of incense.

A Story of Divination

A Story of Divination

~

I ONCE knew a fortune-teller who really believed in the science that he professed. He
had learned, as a student of the old Chinese
philosophy, to believe in divination long before he
thought of practising it. During his youth he
had been in the service of a wealthy daimyō, but
subsequently, like thousands of other samurai,
found himself reduced to desperate straits by the
social and political changes of Meiji. It was then
that he became a fortune-teller, — an itinerant
uranaiya, — travelling on foot from town to
town, and returning to his home rarely more than
once a year with the proceeds of his journey. As
a fortune-teller he was tolerably successful, —
chiefly, I think, because of his perfect sincerity,
and because of a peculiar gentle manner that invited confidence. His system was the old schol-
arly one: he used the book known to English

readers as the *Yî-King*, — also a set of ebony
blocks which could be so arranged as to form
any of the Chinese hexagrams ; — and he always
began his divination with an earnest prayer to
the gods.

The system itself he held to be infallible in
the hands of a master. He confessed that he
had made some erroneous predictions ; but he
said that these mistakes had been entirely due
to his own miscomprehension of certain texts
or diagrams. To do him justice I must mention that in my own case — (he told my fortune
four times), — his predictions were fulfilled in
such wise that I became afraid of them. You
may disbelieve in fortune-telling, — intellectually
scorn it ; but something of inherited superstitious tendency lurks within most of us ; and a
few strange experiences can so appeal to that
inheritance as to induce the most unreasoning
hope or fear of the good or bad luck promised
you by some diviner. Really to see our future
would be a misery. Imagine the result of knowing that there must happen to you, within the
next two months, some terrible misfortune which
you cannot possibly provide against !

He was already an old man when I first saw

him in Izumo, — certainly more than sixty years
of age, but looking very much younger. Afterwards I met him in Ōsaka, in Kyōto, and in
Kobé. More than once I tried to persuade him
to pass the colder months of the winter-season
under my roof, — for he possessed an extraordinary knowledge of traditions, and could have
been of inestimable service to me in a literary way.
But partly because the habit of wandering had
become with him a second nature, and partly
because of a love of independence as savage as a
gipsy's, I was never able to keep him with me for
more than two days at a time.

Every year he used to come to Tōkyō, — usually in the latter part of autumn. Then, for
several weeks, he would flit about the city, from
district to district, and vanish again. But during
these fugitive trips he never failed to visit me;
bringing welcome news of Izumo people and
places, — bringing also some queer little present,
generally of a religious kind, from some famous
place of pilgrimage. On these occasions I could
get a few hours' chat with him. Sometimes the
talk was of strange things seen or heard during
his recent journey; sometimes it turned upon old
legends or beliefs; sometimes it was about for-

tune-telling.   The last time we met he told me of an exact Chinese science of divination which he regretted never having been able to learn.

"Any one learned in that science," he said, "would be able, for example, not only to tell you the exact time at which any post or beam of this house will yield to decay, but even to tell you the direction of the breaking, and all its results.   I can best explain what I mean by relating a story.

" The story is about the famous Chinese fortune-teller whom we call in Japan Shōko Setsu, and it is written in the book *Baikwa-Shin-Eki*, which is a book of divination.   While still a very young man, Shōko Setsu obtained a high position by reason of his learning and virtue; but he resigned it and went into solitude that he might give his whole time to study.   For years thereafter he lived alone in a hut among the mountains; studying without a fire in winter, and without a fan in summer; writing his thoughts upon the wall of his room — for lack of paper; — and using only a tile for his pillow.

"One day, in the period of greatest summer heat, he found himself overcome by drowsiness; and he lay down to rest, with his tile under his head. Scarcely had he fallen asleep when a rat ran across his face and woke him with a start. Feeling angry, he seized his tile and flung it at the rat; but the rat escaped unhurt, and the tile was broken. Shōko Setsu looked sorrowfully at the fragments of his pillow, and reproached himself for his hastiness. Then suddenly he perceived, upon the freshly exposed clay of the broken tile, some Chinese characters — between the upper and lower surfaces. Thinking this very strange, he picked up the pieces, and carefully examined them. He found that along the line of fracture seventeen characters had been written within the clay before the tile had been baked; and the characters read thus: —' *In the Year of the Hare, in the fourth month, on the seventeenth day, at the Hour of the Serpent, this tile, after serving as a pillow, will be thrown at a rat and broken.*' Now the prediction had really been fulfilled at the Hour of the Serpent on the seventeenth day of the fourth month of the Year of the Hare. Greatly astonished, Shōko Setsu once again looked at the fragments, and discovered the seal and the name of the maker. At once he left his hut, and, taking with him the pieces of the tile, hurried to the neighboring town in search of the tilemaker. He found the tilemaker in the course of the day, showed him the broken tile, and asked him about its history.

" After having carefully examined the shards, the tilemaker said : — 'This tile was made in my house; but the characters in the clay were written by an old man — a fortune-teller, — who asked permission to write upon the tile before it was baked.' — 'Do you know where he lives?' asked Shōko Setsu. 'He used to live,' the tile-maker answered, 'not very far from here; and I can show you the way to the house. But I do not know his name.'

" Having been guided to the house, Shōko Setsu presented himself at the entrance, and asked for permission to speak to the old man. A serv-ing-student courteously invited him to enter, and ushered him into an apartment where several young men were at study. As Shōko Setsu took his seat, all the youths saluted him. Then the one who had first addressed him bowed and said : — 'We are grieved to inform you that our master died a few days ago. But we have been wait-ing for you, because he predicted that you would come to-day to this house, at this very hour. Your name is Shōko Setsu. And our master told us to give you a book which he believed would be of service to you.   Here is the book ; — please to accept it.'

" Shōko Setsu was not less delighted than surprised ; for the book was a manuscript of the rarest and most precious kind, — containing all the secrets of the science of divination.   After having thanked the young men, and properly expressed his regret for the death of their teacher, he went back to his hut, and there immediately proceeded to test the worth of the book by consulting its pages in regard to his own fortune. The book suggested to him that on the south side of his dwelling, at a particular spot near one corner of the hut, great luck awaited him.   He dug at the place indicated, and found a jar containing gold enough to make him a very wealthy man."

*
* *

My old acquaintance left this world as lonesomely as he had lived in it.   Last winter, while crossing a mountain-range, he was overtaken by a snowstorm, and lost his way.   Many days later he was found standing erect at the foot of a pine, with his little pack strapped to his shoulders : a statue of ice — arms folded and eyes closed as in meditation. Probably, while waiting for the storm to pass, he had yielded to the drowsiness of cold, and the drift had risen over him as he slept. Hearing of this strange death I remembered the old Japanese saying, — *Uranaiya minouyé shir-adẓu* : "The fortune-teller knows not his own fate."

Silkworms

Silkworms

❧

I

I WAS puzzled by the phrase, "silkworm-moth eyebrow," in an old Japanese, or rather Chinese proverb: — *The silkworm-moth eyebrow of a woman is the axe that cuts down the wisdom of man.* So I went to my friend Niimi, who keeps silkworms, to ask for an explanation.

"Is it possible," he exclaimed, "that you never saw a silkworm-moth? The silkworm-moth has very beautiful eyebrows."

"Eyebrows?" I queried, in astonishment.

"Well, call them what you like," returned Niimi; — "the poets call them eyebrows. . . . Wait a moment, and I will show you."

He left the guest-room, and presently returned with a white paper-fan, on which a silkworm-moth was sleepily reposing.

" We always reserve a few for breeding," he said ; — " this one is just out of the cocoon. It cannot fly, of course : none of them can fly. . . . Now look at the eyebrows."

I looked, and saw that the antennæ, very short and feathery, were so arched back over the two jewel-specks of eyes in the velvety head, as to give the appearance of a really handsome pair of eyebrows.

Then Niimi took me to see his worms.

In Niimi's neighborhood, where there are plenty of mulberry-trees, many families keep silkworms ; — the tending and feeding being mostly done by women and children. The worms are kept in large oblong trays, elevated upon light wooden stands about three feet high. It is curious to see hundreds of caterpillars feeding all together in one tray, and to hear the soft papery noise which they make while gnawing their mulberry-leaves. As they approach maturity, the creatures need almost constant attention. At brief intervals some expert visits each tray to inspect progress, picks up the plumpest feeders, and decides, by gently rolling them between forefinger and thumb, which are ready to spin. These are dropped into covered boxes, where they soon swathe themselves out of sight in white floss. A few only of the best are suffered to emerge from their silky sleep, — the selected breeders. They have beautiful wings, but cannot use them. They have mouths, but do not eat. They only pair, lay eggs, and die. For thousands of years their race has been so well-cared for, that it can no longer take any care of itself.

It was the evolutional lesson of this latter fact that chiefly occupied me while Niimi and his younger brother (who feeds the worms) were kindly explaining the methods of the industry. They told me curious things about different breeds, and also about a wild variety of silkworm that cannot be domesticated : — it spins splendid silk before turning into a vigorous moth which can use its wings to some purpose. But I fear that I did not act like a person who felt interested in the subject ; for, even while I tried to listen, I began to muse.

II

First of all, I found myself thinking about a delightful revery by M. Anatole France, in which he says that if he had been the Demiurge, he would have put youth at the end of life instead of at the beginning, and would have otherwise so ordered matters that every human being should have three stages of development, somewhat corresponding to those of the lepidoptera. Then it occurred to me that this fantasy was in substance scarcely more than the delicate modification of a most ancient doctrine, common to nearly all the higher forms of religion.

Western faiths especially teach that our life on earth is a larval state of greedy helplessness, and that death is a pupa-sleep out of which we should soar into everlasting light. They tell us that during its sentient existence, the outer body should be thought of only as a kind of caterpillar, and thereafter as a chrysalis; — and they aver that we lose or gain, according to our behavior as larvæ, the power to develop wings under the mortal wrapping. Also they tell us not to trouble ourselves about the fact that we see no Psyché-imago detach itself from the broken cocoon: this lack of visual evidence signifies nothing, because we have only the purblind vision of grubs. Our eyes are but half-evolved. Do not whole scales of colors invisibly exist above and below the limits of our retinal sensibility? Even so the butterfly-man exists, — although, as a matter of course, we cannot see him.

But what would become of this human imago in a state of perfect bliss? From the evolutional point of view the question has interest; and its obvious answer was suggested to me by the history of those silkworms, — which have been domesticated for only a few thousand years. Consider the result of our celestial domestication for — let us say — several millions of years: I mean the final consequence, to the wishers, of being able to gratify every wish at will.

Those silkworms have all that they wish for,— even considerably more. Their wants, though very simple, are fundamentally identical with the necessities of mankind, — food, shelter, warmth, safety, and comfort. Our endless social struggle is mainly for these things. Our dream of heaven is the dream of obtaining them free of cost in pain; and the condition of those silkworms is the realization, in a small way, of our imagined Paradise. (I am not considering the fact that a vast majority of the worms are predestined to torment and the second death; for my theme is of heaven, not of lost souls. I am speaking of the elect — those worms preördained to salvation and rebirth.) Probably they can feel only very weak sensations: they are certainly incapable of prayer. But if they were able to pray, they could not ask for anything more than they already receive from the youth who feeds and tends them. He is their providence, — a god of whose existence they can be aware in only the vaguest possible way, but just such a god as they require. And we should foolishly deem ourselves fortunate to be equally well cared-for in proportion to our more complex wants. Do not our common forms of prayer prove our desire for like attention? Is not the assertion of our " need of divine love" an involuntary confession that we wish to be treated like silkworms, — to live without pain by the help of gods? Yet if the gods were to treat us as we want, we should presently afford fresh evidence, — in the way of what is called " the evidence from degeneration," — that the great evolutional law is far above the gods.

An early stage of that degeneration would be represented by total incapacity to help ourselves; — then we should begin to lose the use of our higher sense-organs; — later on, the brain would shrink to a vanishing pin-point of matter; — still later we should dwindle into mere amorphous sacs, mere blind stomachs. Such would be the physical consequence of that kind of divine love which we so lazily wish for. The longing for perpetual bliss in perpetual peace might well seem a malevolent inspiration from the Lords of Death and Darkness. All life that feels and thinks has been, and can continue to be, only as the product of struggle and pain, — only as the outcome of endless battle with the Powers of the Universe. And cosmic law is uncompromising. Whatever organ ceases to know pain, — whatever faculty ceases to be used under the stimulus of pain, — must also cease to exist. Let pain and its effort be suspended, and life must shrink back, first into protoplasmic shapelessness, thereafter into dust.

Buddhism — which, in its own grand way, is a doctrine of evolution — rationally proclaims its heaven but a higher stage of development through pain, and teaches that even in paradise the cessation of effort produces degradation. With equal reasonableness it declares that the capacity for pain in the superhuman world increases always in proportion to the capacity for pleasure. (There is little fault to be found with this teaching from a scientific standpoint, — since we know that higher evolution must involve an increase of sensitivity to pain.) In the Heavens of Desire, says the *Shōbō-nen-jō-kyō*, the pain of death is so great that all the agonies of all the hells united could equal but one-sixteenth part of such pain.[1]

The foregoing comparison is unnecessarily strong; but the Buddhist teaching about heaven is in substance eminently logical. The suppression of pain — mental or physical, — in any conceivable state of sentient existence, would necessarily involve the suppression also of pleasure; — and certainly all progress, whether moral or material,

[1] This statement refers only to the Heavens of Sensuous Pleasure, — not to the Paradise of Amida, nor to those heavens into which one enters by the Apparitional Birth. But even in the highest and most immaterial zones of being, — in the Heavens of Formlessness, — the cessation of effort and of the pain of effort, involves the penalty of rebirth in a lower state of existence.

depends upon the power to meet and to master pain. In a silkworm-paradise such as our mundane instincts lead us to desire, the seraph freed from the necessity of toil, and able to satisfy his every want at will, would lose his wings at last, and sink back to the condition of a grub. . . .

III

I told the substance of my revery to Niimi. He used to be a great reader of Buddhist books.

"Well," he said, " I was reminded of a queer Buddhist story by the proverb that you asked me to explain, — *The silkworm-moth eyebrow of a woman is the axe that cuts down the wisdom of man.* According to our doctrine, the saying would be as true of life in heaven as of life upon earth. . . . This is the story : —

" When Shaka[1] dwelt in this world, one of his disciples, called Nanda, was bewitched by the beauty of a woman ; and Shaka desired to save him from the results of this illusion. So he took

[1] Sâkyamuni.

Nanda to a wild place in the mountains where there were apes, and showed him a very ugly female ape, and asked him : — 'Which is the more beautiful, Nanda, — the woman that you love, or this female ape ? ' 'Oh, Master ! ' exclaimed Nanda, — 'how can a lovely woman be compared with an ugly ape ? ' 'Perhaps you will presently find reason to make the comparison yourself,' answered the Buddha ; — and instantly by supernatural power he ascended with Nanda to the *Sanjūsan-Ten*, which is the Second of the Six Heavens of Desire. There, within a palace of jewels, Nanda saw a multitude of heavenly maidens celebrating some festival with music and dance ; and the beauty of the least among them incomparably exceeded that of the fairest woman of earth. 'O Master,' cried Nanda, 'what wonderful festival is this ? ' 'Ask some of those people,' responded Shaka. So Nanda questioned one of the celestial maidens ; and she said to him : — 'This festival is to celebrate the good tidings that have been brought to us. There is now in the human world, among the disciples of Shaka, a most excellent youth called Nanda, who is soon to be reborn into this heaven, and to become our bridegroom, because of his holy life. We wait for him with rejoicing.' This reply filled the heart of Nanda with delight. Then the Buddha asked him : — ' Is there any one among these maidens, Nanda, equal in beauty to the woman with whom you have been in love ? ' ' Nay, Master ! ' answered Nanda ; — ' even as that woman surpassed in beauty the female ape that we saw on the mountain, so is she herself surpassed by even the least among these.'

" Then the Buddha immediately descended with Nanda to the depths of the hells, and took him into a torture-chamber where myriads of men and women were being boiled alive in great caldrons, and otherwise horribly tormented by devils. Then Nanda found himself standing before a huge vessel which was filled with molten metal ; — and he feared and wondered because this vessel had as yet no occupant. An idle devil sat beside it, yawning. ' Master,' Nanda inquired of the Buddha, ' for whom has this vessel been prepared ? ' ' Ask the devil,' answered Shaka. Nanda did so ; and the devil said to him : — ' There is a man called Nanda, — now one of Shaka's disciples, — about to be reborn into one of the heavens, on account of his former good actions. But after having there indulged himself, he is to be reborn

in this hell; and his place will be in that pot.   I
am waiting for him.' " [1]

[1] I give the story substantially as it was told to me; but I
have not been able to compare it with any published text.
My friend says that he has seen two Chinese versions, —
one in the *Hongyō-kyō* (?), the other in the *Zōichi-agon-kyō*
(Ekôttarâgamas).   In Mr. Henry Clarke Warren's *Buddhism in
Translations* (the most interesting and valuable single volume
of its kind that I have ever seen), there is a Pali version of
the legend, which differs considerably from the above. —
This Nanda, according to Mr. Warren's work, was a prince,
and the younger half-brother of Sâkyamuni.

A Passional Karma

A Passional Karma

❦

ONE of the never-failing attractions of the Tōkyō stage is the performance, by the famous Kikugorō and his company, of the *Botan-Dōrō*, or "Peony-Lantern." This weird play, of which the scenes are laid in the middle of the last century, is the dramatization of a romance by the novelist Enchō, written in colloquial Japanese, and purely Japanese in local color, though inspired by a Chinese tale. I went to see the play ; and Kikugorō made me familiar with a new variety of the pleasure of fear.

"Why not give English readers the ghostly part of the story ? " — asked a friend who guides me betimes through the mazes of Eastern philosophy. "It would serve to explain some popular ideas of the supernatural which Western people know very little about. And I could help you with the translation."

I gladly accepted the suggestion ; and we composed the following summary of the more extraordinary portion of Enchō's romance. Here and there we found it necessary to condense the original narrative ; and we tried to keep close to the text only in the conversational passages, — some of which happen to possess a particular quality of psychological interest.

*
* *

— This is the story of the Ghosts in the Romance of the Peony-Lantern : —

I

There once lived in the district of Ushigomé, in Yedo, a *hatamoto* [1] called Iijima Heizayémon, whose only daughter, Tsuyu, was beautiful as her name, which signifies " Morning Dew." Iijima took a second wife when his daughter was about sixteen ; and, finding that O-Tsuyu

[1] The *hatamoto* were samurai forming the special military force of the Shōgun. The name literally signifies " Banner-Supporters." These were the highest class of samurai, — not only as the immediate vassals of the Shōgun, but as a military aristocracy.

could not be happy with her mother-in-law, he had a pretty villa built for the girl at Yanagijima, as a separate residence, and gave her an excellent maidservant, called O-Yoné, to wait upon her.

O-Tsuyu lived happily enough in her new home until one day when the family physician, Yamamoto Shijō, paid her a visit in company with a young samurai named Hagiwara Shinzaburō, who resided in the Nedzu quarter. Shinzaburō was an unusually handsome lad, and very gentle; and the two young people fell in love with each other at sight. Even before the brief visit was over, they contrived, — unheard by the old doctor, — to pledge themselves to each other for life. And, at parting, O-Tsuyu whispered to the youth, — "*Remember! if you do not come to see me again, I shall certainly die!*"

Shinzaburō never forgot those words; and he was only too eager to see more of O-Tsuyu. But etiquette forbade him to make the visit alone: he was obliged to wait for some other chance to accompany the doctor, who had promised to take him to the villa a second time. Unfortunately the old man did not keep this promise. He had perceived the sudden affection of O-Tsuyu; and he feared that her father would hold him responsible for any serious results. Iijima Heizayémon had a reputation for cutting off heads. And the more Shijō thought about the possible consequences of his introduction of Shinzaburō at the Iijima villa, the more he became afraid. Therefore he purposely abstained from calling upon his young friend.

Months passed; and O-Tsuyu, little imagining the true cause of Shinzaburō's neglect, believed that her love had been scorned. Then she pined away, and died. Soon afterwards, the faithful servant O-Yoné also died, through grief at the loss of her mistress; and the two were buried side by side in the cemetery of Shin-Banzui-In,— a temple which still stands in the neighborhood of Dango-Zaka, where the famous chrysanthemum-shows are yearly held.

II

Shinzaburō knew nothing of what had happened; but his disappointment and his anxiety had resulted in a prolonged illness. He was slowly recovering, but still very weak, when he unexpectedly received another visit from Yamamoto Shijō. The old man made a number of plausible excuses for his apparent neglect. Shinzaburō said to him : —

" I have been sick ever since the beginning of spring ; — even now I cannot eat anything. . . . Was it not rather unkind of you never to call ? I thought that we were to make another visit together to the house of the Lady Iijima; and I wanted to take to her some little present as a return for our kind reception. Of course I could not go by myself."

Shijo gravely responded, —

" I am very sorry to tell you that the young lady is dead."

"Dead ! " repeated Shinzaburō, turning white, — " did you say that she is dead ? "

The doctor remained silent for a moment, as if collecting himself : then he resumed, in the quick light tone of a man resolved not to take trouble seriously : —

" My great mistake was in having introduced you to her ; for it seems that she fell in love with you at once. I am afraid that you must have said something to encourage this affection —

when you were in that little room together. At all events, I saw how she felt towards you; and then I became uneasy, — fearing that her father might come to hear of the matter, and lay the whole blame upon me. So — to be quite frank with you, — I decided that it would be better not to call upon you; and I purposely stayed away for a long time. But, only a few days ago, happening to visit Iijima's house, I heard, to my great surprise, that his daughter had died, and that her servant O-Yoné had also died. Then, remembering all that had taken place, I knew that the young lady must have died of love for you. . . . [*Laughing*] Ah, you are really a sinful fellow! Yes, you are! [*Laughing*] Is n't it a sin to have been born so handsome that the girls die for love of you?[1] . . . [*Seriously*] Well, we must leave the dead to the dead. It is no use to talk further about the matter; — all that you now can do for her is to repeat the Nembutsu[2] . . . Good-bye."

[1] Perhaps this conversation may seem strange to the Western reader; but it is true to life. The whole of the scene is characteristically Japanese.

[2] The invocation *Namu Amida Butsu!* ("Hail to the Buddha Amitâbha!"), — repeated, as a prayer, for the sake of the dead.

And the old man retired hastily, — anxious to avoid further converse about the painful event for which he felt himself to have been unwittingly responsible.

III

Shinzaburō long remained stupefied with grief by the news of O-Tsuyu's death. But as soon as he found himself again able to think clearly, he inscribed the dead girl's name upon a mortuary tablet, and placed the tablet in the Buddhist shrine of his house, and set offerings before it, and recited prayers. Every day thereafter he presented offerings, and repeated the *Nembutsu;* and the memory of O-Tsuyu was never absent from his thought.

Nothing occurred to change the monotony of his solitude before the time of the Bon, — the great Festival of the Dead, — which begins upon the thirteenth day of the seventh month. Then he decorated his house, and prepared everything for the festival ; — hanging out the lanterns that guide the returning spirits, and setting the food of ghosts on the *shōryōdana,* or Shelf of Souls.

And on the first evening of the Bon, after sundown, he kindled a small lamp before the tablet of O-Tsuyu, and lighted the lanterns.

The night was clear, with a great moon, — and windless, and very warm. Shinzaburō sought the coolness of his veranda. Clad only in a light summer-robe, he sat there thinking, dreaming, sorrowing; — sometimes fanning himself; sometimes making a little smoke to drive the mosquitoes away. Everything was quiet. It was a lonesome neighborhood, and there were few passers-by. He could hear only the soft rushing of a neighboring stream, and the shrilling of night-insects.

But all at once this stillness was broken by a sound of women's *geta* [1] approaching — *kara-kon, kara-kon;* — and the sound drew nearer and nearer, quickly, till it reached the live-hedge surrounding the garden. Then Shinzaburō, feeling curious, stood on tiptoe, so as to look over the hedge; and he saw two women passing. One, who was carrying a beautiful lantern deco-

---

[1] *Komageta* in the original. The geta is a wooden sandal, or clog, of which there are many varieties, — some decidedly elegant. The *komageta*, or "pony-geta" is so-called because of the sonorous hoof-like echo which it makes on hard ground.

THE PEONY LANTERN

rated with peony-flowers,[1] appeared to be a servant; — the other was a slender girl of about seventeen, wearing a long-sleeved robe embroidered with designs of autumn-blossoms. Almost at the same instant both women turned their faces toward Shinzaburō; — and to his utter astonishment, he recognized O-Tsuyu and her servant O-Yoné.

They stopped immediately; and the girl cried out, —

"Oh, how strange! . . . Hagiwara Sama!"

Shinzaburō simultaneously called to the maid: —

"O-Yoné! Ah, you are O-Yoné! — I remember you very well."

"Hagiwara Sama!" exclaimed O-Yoné in a tone of supreme amazement. "Never could I have believed it possible! . . . Sir, we were told that you had died."

---

[1] The sort of lantern here referred to is no longer made; and its shape can best be understood by a glance at the picture accompanying this story. It was totally unlike the modern domestic hand-lantern, painted with the owner's crest; but it was not altogether unlike some forms of lanterns still manufactured for the Festival of the Dead, and called *Bon-dōrō*. The flowers ornamenting it were not painted: they were artificial flowers of crêpe-silk, and were attached to the top of the lantern.

"How extraordinary!" cried Shinzaburō. "Why, I was told that both of you were dead!"

"Ah, what a hateful story!" returned O-Yoné. "Why repeat such unlucky words? . . . Who told you?"

"Please to come in," said Shinzaburō; — "here we can talk better. The garden-gate is open."

So they entered, and exchanged greeting; and when Shinzaburō had made them comfortable, he said: —

"I trust that you will pardon my discourtesy in not having called upon you for so long a time. But Shijō, the doctor, about a month ago, told me that you had both died."

"So it was he who told you?" exclaimed O-Yoné. "It was very wicked of him to say such a thing. Well, it was also Shijō who told us that *you* were dead. I think that he wanted to deceive you, — which was not a difficult thing to do, because you are so confiding and trustful. Possibly my mistress betrayed her liking for you in some words which found their way to her father's ears; and, in that case, O-Kuni — the new wife — might have planned to make the doctor tell you that we were dead, so as to bring

about a separation.   Anyhow, when my mistress
heard that you had died, she wanted to cut off
her hair immediately, and to become a nun.   But
I was able to prevent her from cutting off her
hair; and I persuaded her at last to become a
nun only in her heart.   Afterwards her father
wished her to marry a certain young man ; and
she refused.   Then there was a great deal of
trouble, — chiefly caused by O-Kuni ; — and we
went away from the villa, and found a very
small house in Yanaka-no-Sasaki.   There we are
now just barely able to live, by doing a little
private work. . . .   My mistress has been constantly repeating the *Nembutsu* for your sake.
To-day, being the first day of the Bon, we went
to visit the temples; and we were on our way
home — thus late — when this strange meeting
happened."

" Oh, how extraordinary ! " cried Shinzaburō.
" Can it be true ? — or is it only a dream ?   Here
I, too, have been constantly reciting the *Nem-
butsu* before a tablet with her name upon it !
Look ! "   And he showed them O-Tsuyu's
tablet in its place upon the Shelf of Souls.

" We are more than grateful for your kind
remembrance," returned O-Yoné, smiling. . . .

" Now as for my mistress," — she continued, turning towards O-Tsuyu, who had all the while remained demure and silent, half-hiding her face with her sleeve, — " as for my mistress, she actually says that she would not mind being disowned by her father for the time of seven existences,[1] or even being killed by him, for your sake!
. . . Come! will you not allow her to stay here to-night ? "

Shinzaburō turned pale for joy. He answered in a voice trembling with emotion : —

" Please remain ; but do not speak loud — because there is a troublesome fellow living close by, — a *ninsomi*[2] called Hakuōdō Yusai, who tells people's fortunes by looking at their faces. He is inclined to be curious ; and it is better that he should not know."

---

[1] " For the time of seven existences," — that is to say, for the time of seven successive lives. In Japanese drama and romance it is not uncommon to represent a father as disowning his child " for the time of seven lives." Such a disowning is called *shichi-shō madé no mandō*, a disinheritance for seven lives, — signifying that in six future lives after the present the erring son or daughter will continue to feel the parental displeasure.

[2] The profession is not yet extinct. The *ninsomi* uses a kind of magnifying glass (or magnifying-mirror sometimes), called *tengankyō* or *ninsomégané*.

The two women remained that night in the house of the young samurai, and returned to their own home a little before daybreak. And after that night they came every night for seven nights, — whether the weather were foul or fair, — always at the same hour. And Shinzaburō became more and more attached to the girl; and the twain were fettered, each to each, by that bond of illusion which is stronger than bands of iron.

IV

Now there was a man called Tomozō, who lived in a small cottage adjoining Shinzaburō's residence. Tomozō and his wife O-Miné were both employed by Shinzaburō as servants. Both seemed to be devoted to their young master; and by his help they were able to live in comparative comfort.

One night, at a very late hour, Tomozō heard the voice of a woman in his master's apartment; and this made him uneasy. He feared that Shinzaburō, being very gentle and affectionate, might be made the dupe of some cunning wanton, — in which event the domestics would be the first to suffer. He therefore resolved to watch; and on the following night he stole on tiptoe to Shinzaburō's dwelling, and looked through a chink in one of the sliding shutters. By the glow of a night-lantern within the sleeping-room, he was able to perceive that his master and a strange woman were talking together under the mosquito-net. At first he could not see the woman distinctly. Her back was turned to him; — he only observed that she was very slim, and that she appeared to be very young, — judging from the fashion of her dress and hair.[1] Putting his ear to the chink, he could hear the conversation plainly. The woman said: —

"And if I should be disowned by my father, would you then let me come and live with you?"

Shinzaburō answered: —

"Most assuredly I would — nay, I should be glad of the chance. But there is no reason to fear that you will ever be disowned by your father; for you are his only daughter, and he loves you very much. What I do fear is that some day we shall be cruelly separated."

---

[1] The color and form of the dress, and the style of wearing the hair, are by Japanese custom regulated according to the age of the woman.

She responded softly : —

" Never, never could I even think of accepting any other man for my husband. Even if our secret were to become known, and my father were to kill me for what I have done, still — after death itself — I could never cease to think of you. And I am now quite sure that you yourself would not be able to live very long without me." . . . Then clinging closely to him, with her lips at his neck, she caressed him ; and he returned her caresses.

Tomozō wondered as he listened, — because the language of the woman was not the language of a common woman, but the language of a lady of rank.[1] Then he determined at all hazards to get one glimpse of her face ; and he crept round the house, backwards and forwards, peering through every crack and chink. And at last he was able to see ; — but therewith an icy trembling seized him ; and the hair of his head stood up.

For the face was the face of a woman long

[1] The forms of speech used by the samurai, and other superior classes, differed considerably from those of the popular idiom ; but these differences could not be effectively rendered into English.

dead, — and the fingers caressing were fingers of naked bone, — and of the body below the waist there was not anything : it melted off into thinnest trailing shadow. Where the eyes of the lover deluded saw youth and grace and beauty, there appeared to the eyes of the watcher horror only, and the emptiness of death. Simultaneously another woman's figure, and a weirder, rose up from within the chamber, and swiftly made toward the watcher, as if discerning his presence. Then, in uttermost terror, he fled to the dwelling of Hakuōdō Yusai, and, knocking frantically at the doors, succeeded in arousing him.

V

Hakuōdō Yusai, the *ninsomi*, was a very old man ; but in his time he had travelled much, and he had heard and seen so many things that he could not be easily surprised. Yet the story of the terrified Tomozō both alarmed and amazed him. He had read in ancient Chinese books of love between the living and the dead ; but he had never believed it possible. Now, however, he felt convinced that the statement of Tomozō was not a falsehood, and that something very strange was really going on in the house of Hagiwara. Should the truth prove to be what Tomozō imagined, then the young samurai was a doomed man.

" If the woman be a ghost," — said Yusai to the frightened servant, " — if the woman be a ghost, your master must die very soon, — unless something extraordinary can be done to save him. And if the woman be a ghost, the signs of death will appear upon his face. For the spirit of the living is *yōki*, and pure ; — the spirit of the dead is *inki*, and unclean : the one is Positive, the other Negative. He whose bride is a ghost cannot live. Even though in his blood there existed the force of a life of one hundred years, that force must quickly perish. . . . Still, I shall do all that I can to save Hagiwara Sama. And in the meantime, Tomozō, say nothing to any other person, — not even to your wife, — about this matter. At sunrise I shall call upon your master."

VI

When questioned next morning by Yusai, Shin-zaburō at first attempted to deny that any women had been visiting the house; but finding this artless policy of no avail, and perceiving that the old man's purpose was altogether unselfish, he was finally persuaded to acknowledge what had really occurred, and to give his reasons for wishing to keep the matter a secret. As for the lady Iijima, he intended, he said, to make her his wife as soon as possible.

" Oh, madness ! " cried Yusai, — losing all patience in the intensity of his alarm. " Know, sir, that the people who have been coming here, night after night, are dead ! Some frightful delusion is upon you ! . . . Why, the simple fact that you long supposed O-Tsuyu to be dead, and repeated the *Nembutsu* for her, and made offerings before her tablet, is itself the proof ! . . . The lips of the dead have touched you ! — the hands of the dead have caressed you ! . . . Even at this moment I see in your face the signs of death — and you will not believe ! . . . Listen to me now, sir, — I beg of you, — if you wish to save yourself: otherwise you have less than twenty days to live. They told you — those people — that they were residing in the district of Shitaya, in Yanaka-no-Sasaki. Did you ever visit them at that place? No! — of course you did not! Then go to-day, — as soon as you can, — to Yanaka-no-Sasaki, and try to find their home! . . . "

And having uttered this counsel with the most vehement earnestness, Hakuōdō Yusai abruptly took his departure.

Shinzaburō, startled though not convinced, re-solved after a moment's reflection to follow the advice of the *ninsomi*, and to go to Shitaya. It was yet early in the morning when he reached the quarter of Yanaka-no-Sasaki, and began his search for the dwelling of O-Tsuyu. He went through every street and side-street, read all the names inscribed at the various entrances, and made in-quiries whenever an opportunity presented itself. But he could not find anything resembling the little house mentioned by O-Yoné ; and none of the people whom he questioned knew of any house in the quarter inhabited by two single women. Feeling at last certain that further

research would be useless, he turned homeward
by the shortest way, which happened to lead
through the grounds of the temple Shin-Banzui-In.

Suddenly his attention was attracted by two
new tombs, placed side by side, at the rear of
the temple. One was a common tomb, such as
might have been erected for a person of humble
rank : the other was a large and handsome monument ; and hanging before it was a beautiful
peony-lantern, which had probably been left there
at the time of the Festival of the Dead. Shinzaburō remembered that the peony-lantern carried
by O-Yoné was exactly similar ; and the coin-
cidence impressed him as strange. He looked
again at the tombs ; but the tombs explained
nothing. Neither bore any personal name, —
only the Buddhist *kaimyō*, or posthumous appel-
lation. Then he determined to seek information
at the temple. An acolyte stated, in reply to his
questions, that the large tomb had been recently
erected for the daughter of Iijima Heizayemon,
the *hatamoto* of Ushigomé ; and that the small
tomb next to it was that of her servant O-Yoné,
who had died of grief soon after the young lady's
funeral.

Immediately to Shinzaburō's memory there recurred, with another and sinister meaning, the words of O-Yoné : — "*We went away, and found a very small house in Yanaka-no-Sasaki. There we are now just barely able to live — by doing a little private work. . . .*" Here was indeed the very small house, — and in Yanaka-no-Sasaki. But the little *private work* . . . ?

Terror-stricken, the samurai hastened with all speed to the house of Yusai, and begged for his counsel and assistance. But Yusai declared himself unable to be of any aid in such a case. All that he could do was to send Shinzaburō to the high-priest Ryōseki, of Shin-Banzui-In, with a letter praying for immediate religious help.

VII

The high-priest Ryōseki was a learned and a holy man. By spiritual vision he was able to know the secret of any sorrow, and the nature of the karma that had caused it. He heard unmoved the story of Shinzaburō, and said to him : —

" A very great danger now threatens you, because of an error committed in one of your former states of existence. The karma that binds you to the dead is very strong; but if I tried to explain its character, you would not be able to understand. I shall therefore tell you only this, — that the dead person has no desire to injure you out of hate, feels no enmity towards you: she is influenced, on the contrary, by the most passionate affection for you. Probably the girl has been in love with you from a time long preceding your present life, — from a time of not less than three or four past existences; and it would seem that, although necessarily changing her form and condition at each succeeding birth, she has not been able to cease from following after you. Therefore it will not be an easy thing to escape from her influence. . . . But now I am going to lend you this powerful *mamori*.[1] It is a pure gold image of that Buddha

[1] The Japanese word *mamori* has significations at least as numerous as those attaching to our own term " amulet." It would be impossible, in a mere footnote, even to suggest the variety of Japanese religious objects to which the name is given. In this instance, the *mamori* is a very small image, probably enclosed in a miniature shrine of lacquerwork or metal, over which a silk cover is drawn. Such

called the Sea-Sounding Tathâgata — *Kai-On-Nyōrai*, — because his preaching of the Law sounds through the world like the sound of the sea. And this little image is especially a *shiryō-yoké*,[1] — which protects the living from the dead. This you must wear, in its covering, next to your body, — under the girdle. . . . Besides, I shall presently perform in the temple, a *segaki*-service [2] for the repose of the troubled spirit. . . . And here is a holy sutra, called *Ubō-Darani-Kyō*, or "Treasure-Raining Sutra:"[3] you must be

little images were often worn by *samurai* on the person. I was recently shown a miniature figure of Kwannon, in an iron case, which had been carried by an officer through the Satsuma war. He observed, with good reason, that it had probably saved his life; for it had stopped a bullet of which the dent was plainly visible.

[1] From *shiryō*, a ghost, and *yokeru*, to exclude. The Japanese have two kinds of ghosts proper in their folk-lore: the spirits of the dead, *shiryō*; and the spirits of the living, *ikiryō*. A house or a person may be haunted by an *ikiryō* as well as by a *shiryō*.

[2] A special service, — accompanying offerings of food, etc., to those dead having no living relatives or friends to care for them, — is thus termed. In this case, however, the service would be of a particular and exceptional kind.

[3] The name would be more correctly written *Ubō-Darani-Kyō*. It is the Japanese pronunciation of the title of a very short sutra translated out of Sanscrit into Chinese by the Indian priest Amoghavajra, probably during the

careful to recite it every night in your house —
without fail. . . . Furthermore I shall give you
this package of *o-fuda*;[1] — you must paste one
of them over every opening of your house, —
no matter how small. If you do this, the power
of the holy texts will prevent the dead from entering. But — whatever may happen — do not
fail to recite the sutra."

Shinzaburō humbly thanked the high-priest;
and then, taking with him the image, the sutra,
and the bundle of sacred texts, he made all haste
to reach his home before the hour of sunset.

eighth century. The Chinese text contains transliterations
of some mysterious Sanscrit words, — apparently talismanic
words, — like those to be seen in Kern's translation of
the Saddharma-Pundarika, ch. xxvi.

[1] *O-fuda* is the general name given to religious texts
used as charms or talismans. They are sometimes stamped
or burned upon wood, but more commonly written or
printed upon narrow strips of paper. *O-fuda* are pasted
above house-entrances, on the walls of rooms, upon tablets
placed in household shrines, etc., etc. Some kinds are
worn about the person; — others are made into pellets,
and swallowed as spiritual medicine. The text of the
larger *o-fuda* is often accompanied by curious pictures or
symbolic illustrations.

VIII

With Yusai's advice and help, Shinzaburō was able before dark to fix the holy texts over all the apertures of his dwelling. Then the *ninsomi* returned to his own house, — leaving the youth alone.

Night came, warm and clear. Shinzaburō made fast the doors, bound the precious amulet about his waist, entered his mosquito-net, and by the glow of a night-lantern began to recite the *Ubō-Darani-Kyō*. For a long time he chanted the words, comprehending little of their meaning; — then he tried to obtain some rest. But his mind was still too much disturbed by the strange events of the day. Midnight passed; and no sleep came to him. At last he heard the boom of the great temple-bell of Dentsu-In announcing the eighth hour.[1]

[1] According to the old Japanese way of counting time, this *yatsudoki* or eighth hour was the same as our two o'clock in the morning. Each Japanese hour was equal to two European hours, so that there were only six hours instead of our twelve; and these six hours were counted backwards in the order, — 9, 8, 7, 6, 5, 4. Thus the ninth hour corresponded to our midday, or midnight;

It ceased; and Shinzaburō suddenly heard the sound of *geta* approaching from the old direction, — but this time more slowly: *karan-koron, karan-koron!* At once a cold sweat broke over his forehead. Opening the sutra hastily, with trembling hand, he began again to recite it aloud. The steps came nearer and nearer, — reached the live hedge, — stopped! Then, strange to say, Shinzaburō felt unable to remain under his mosquito-net: something stronger even than his fear impelled him to look; and, instead of continuing to recite the *Ubō-Darani-Kyō*, he foolishly approached the shutters, and through a chink peered out into the night. Before the house he saw O-Tsuyu standing, and O-Yoné with the peony-lantern; and both of them were gazing at the Buddhist texts pasted above the entrance. Never before — not even in what time she lived — had O-Tsuyu appeared so beautiful; and Shinzaburō felt his heart drawn towards her with a power almost resistless. But the terror of death

half-past nine to our one o'clock; eight to our two o'clock. Two o'clock in the morning, also called "the Hour of the Ox," was the Japanese hour of ghosts and goblins.

and the terror of the unknown restrained; and there went on within him such a struggle between his love and his fear that he became as one suffering in the body the pains of the Shō-netsu hell.[1]

Presently he heard the voice of the maid-servant, saying: —

" My dear mistress, there is no way to enter. The heart of Hagiwara Sama must have changed. For the promise that he made last night has been broken; and the doors have been made fast to keep us out. . . . We cannot go in to-night. . . . It will be wiser for you to make up your mind not to think any more about him, because his feeling towards you has certainly changed. It is evident that he does not want to see you. So it will be better not to give yourself any more trouble for the sake of a man whose heart is so unkind."

But the girl answered, weeping: —

" Oh, to think that this could happen after the pledges which we made to each other! . . .

---

[1] *En-netsu* or *Shō-netsu* (Sanscrit " Tapana ") is the sixth of the Eight Hot Hells of Japanese Buddhism. One day of life in this hell is equal in duration to thousands (some say millions) of human years.

Often I was told that the heart of a man changes as quickly as the sky of autumn ; — yet surely the heart of Hagiwara Sama cannot be so cruel that he should really intend to exclude me in this way ! . . . Dear Yoné, please find some means of taking me to him. . . . Unless you do, I will never, never go home again."

Thus she continued to plead, veiling her face with her long sleeves, — and very beautiful she looked, and very touching ; but the fear of death was strong upon her lover.

O-Yoné at last made answer, —

" My dear young lady, why will you trouble your mind about a man who seems to be so cruel ? . . . Well, let us see if there be no way to enter at the back of the house : come with me ! "

And taking O-Tsuyu by the hand, she led her away toward the rear of the dwelling ; and there the two disappeared as suddenly as the light disappears when the flame of a lamp is blown out.

IX

Night after night the shadows came at the Hour of the Ox; and nightly Shinzaburō heard the weeping of O-Tsuyu. Yet he believed himself saved, — little imagining that his doom had already . been decided by the character of his dependents.

Tomozō had promised Yusai never to speak to any other person — not even to O-Miné — of the strange events that were taking place. But Tomozō was not long suffered by the haunters to rest in peace. Night after night O-Yoné entered into his dwelling, and roused him from his sleep, and asked him to remove the *o-fuda* placed over one very small window at the back of his master's house. And Tomozō, out of fear, as often promised her to take away the *o-fuda* before the next sundown; but never by day could he make up his mind to remove it, — believing that evil was intended to Shinzaburō. At last, in a night of storm, O-Yoné startled him from slumber with a cry of reproach, and stooped above his pillow, and said to him : " Have a care how you trifle with us! If, by to-morrow night, you do not take away that text, you shall learn how I can hate!" And she made her face so frightful as she spoke that Tomozō nearly died of terror.

O-Miné, the wife of Tomozō, had never till then known of these visits: even to her husband they had seemed like bad dreams. But on this particular night it chanced that, waking suddenly, she heard the voice of a woman talking to Tomozō. Almost in the same moment the talking ceased; and when O-Miné looked about her, she saw, by the light of the night-lamp, only her husband, — shuddering and white with fear. The stranger was gone; the doors were fast: it seemed impossible that anybody could have entered. Nevertheless the jealousy of the wife had been aroused; and she began to chide and to question Tomozō in such a manner that he thought himself obliged to betray the secret, and to explain the terrible dilemma in which he had been placed.

Then the passion of O-Miné yielded to wonder and alarm; but she was a subtle woman, and she devised immediately a plan to save her husband by the sacrifice of her master. And she gave

Tomozō a cunning counsel, — telling him to make conditions with the dead.

They came again on the following night at the Hour of the Ox; and O-Miné hid herself on hearing the sound of their coming, — *karan-koron, karan-koron!* But Tomozō went out to meet them in the dark, and even found courage to say to them what his wife had told him to say : —

" It is true that I deserve your blame ; — but I had no wish to cause you anger. The reason that the *o-fuda* has not been taken away is that my wife and I are able to live only by the help of Hagiwara Sama, and that we cannot expose him to any danger without bringing misfortune upon ourselves. But if we could obtain the sum of a hundred *ryō* in gold, we should be able to please you, because we should then need no help from anybody. Therefore if you will give us a hundred *ryō*, I can take the *o-fuda* away without being afraid of losing our only means of support."

When he had uttered these words, O-Yoné and O-Tsuyu looked at each other in silence for a moment. Then O-Yoné said : —

" Mistress, I told you that it was not right to trouble this man, — as we have no just cause of ill will against him. But it is certainly useless to fret yourself about Hagiwara Sama, because his heart has changed towards you. Now once again, my dear young lady, let me beg you not to think any more about him ! "

But O-Tsuyu, weeping, made answer : —

" Dear Yoné, whatever may happen, I cannot possibly keep myself from thinking about him ! . . . You know that you can get a hundred *ryō* to have the *o-fuda* taken off. . . Only once more, I pray, dear Yoné ! — only once more bring me face to face with Hagiwara Sama, — I beseech you ! " And hiding her face with her sleeve, she thus continued to plead.

" Oh ! why will you ask me to do these things ? " responded O-Yoné. " You know very well that I have no money. But since you will persist in this whim of yours, in spite of all that I can say, I suppose that I must try to find the money somehow, and to bring it here to-morrow night. . . ." Then, turning to the faithless To-mozō, she said : — " Tomozō, I must tell you that Hagiwara Sama now wears upon his body a *mamori* called by the name of *Kai-On-Nyōrai*, and that so long as he wears it we cannot approach him. So you will have to get that *mamori* away from him, by some means or other, as well as to remove the *o-fuda*."

Tomozō feebly made answer : —

" That also I can do, if you will promise to bring me the hundred *ryō*."

" Well, mistress," said O-Yoné, "you will wait, — will you not, — until to-morrow night ? "

" Oh, dear Yoné ! " sobbed the other, — " have we to go back to-night again without seeing Hagiwara Sama ?   Ah ! it is cruel ! "

And the shadow of the mistress, weeping, was led away by the shadow of the maid.

X

Another day went, and another night came, and the dead came with it. But this time no lamentation was heard without the house of Hagiwara ; for the faithless servant found his reward at the Hour of the Ox, and removed the *o-fuda*. Moreover he had been able, while his master was at the bath, to steal from its case the golden *mamori*, and to substitute for it an image of copper; and he had buried the *Kai-On-Ny-ōrai* in a desolate field. So the visitants found nothing to oppose their entering. Veiling their faces with their sleeves they rose and passed, like a streaming of vapor, into the little window from over which the holy text had been torn away. But what happened thereafter within the house Tomozō never knew.

The sun was high before he ventured again to approach his master's dwelling, and to knock upon the sliding-doors. For the first time in years he obtained no response; and the silence made him afraid. Repeatedly he called, and received no answer. Then, aided by O-Miné, he succeeded in effecting an entrance and making his way alone to the sleeping-room, where he called again in vain. He rolled back the rumbling shutters to admit the light; but still within the house there was no stir. At last he dared to lift a corner of the mosquito-net. But no sooner had he looked beneath than he fled from the house, with a cry of horror.

Shinzaburō was dead — hideously dead; — and his face was the face of a man who had died in the uttermost agony of fear; — and lying beside him in the bed were the bones of a woman!

And the bones of the arms, and the bones of the hands, clung fast about his neck.

XI

Hakuōdō Yusai, the fortune-teller, went to view the corpse at the prayer of the faithless Tomozō. The old man was terrified and astonished at the spectacle, but looked about him with a keen eye. He soon perceived that the *o-fuda* had been taken from the little window at the back of the house; and on searching the body of Shinzaburō, he discovered that the golden *mamori* had been taken from its wrapping, and a copper image of Fudō put in place of it. He suspected Tomozō of the theft; but the whole occurrence was so very extraordinary that he thought it prudent to consult with the priest Ryōseki before taking further action. Therefore, after having made a careful examination of the premises, he betook himself to the temple Shin-Banzui-In, as quickly as his aged limbs could bear him.

Ryōseki, without waiting to hear the purpose of the old man's visit, at once invited him into a private apartment.

" You know that you are always welcome here," said Ryōseki. " Please seat yourself at ease. . . . Well, I am sorry to tell you that Hagiwara Sama is dead."

Yusai wonderingly exclaimed : —

" Yes, he is dead ; — but how did you learn of it ? "

The priest responded : —

" Hagiwara Sama was suffering from the results of an evil karma ; and his attendant was a bad man. What happened to Hagiwara Sama was unavoidable ; — his destiny had been determined from a time long before his last birth. It will be better for you not to let your mind be troubled by this event."

Yusai said : —

" I have heard that a priest of pure life may gain power to see into the future for a hundred years ; but truly this is the first time in my existence that I have had proof of such power. . . . Still, there is another matter about which I am very anxious. . . ."

" You mean," interrupted Ryōseki, " the stealing of the holy *mamori*, the *Kai-On-Nyōrai*. But you must not give yourself any concern about that. The image has been buried in a field; and it will be found there and returned to me during the eighth month of the coming year. So please do not be anxious about it."

More and more amazed, the old *ninsomi* ventured to observe: —

" I have studied the *In-Yō*,[1] and the science of divination; and I make my living by telling peoples' fortunes; — but I cannot possibly understand how you know these things."

Ryōseki answered gravely: —

" Never mind how I happen to know them. . . . I now want to speak to you about Hagiwara's funeral. The House of Hagiwara has its own family-cemetery, of course; but to bury him there would not be proper. He must be buried beside O-Tsuyu, the Lady Iijima; for his karma-relation to her was a very deep one. And it is but right that you should erect a tomb for him at your own cost, because you have been indebted to him for many favors."

---

[1] The Male and Female principles of the universe, the Active and Passive forces of Nature. Yusai refers here to the old Chinese nature-philosophy, — better known to Western readers by the name FENG-SHUI.

Thus it came to pass that Shinzaburō was buried beside O-Tsuyu, in the cemetery of Shin-Banzui-In, in Yanaka-no-Sasaki.

— Here ends the story of the Ghosts in the Romance of the Peony-Lantern.

*
* *

My friend asked me whether the story had interested me; and I answered by telling him that I wanted to go to the cemetery of Shin-Banzui-In, — so as to realize more definitely the local color of the author's studies.

"I shall go with you at once," he said. "But what did you think of the personages?"

"To Western thinking," I made answer, "Shinzaburō is a despicable creature. I have been mentally comparing him with the true lovers of our old ballad-literature. They were only too glad to follow a dead sweetheart into the grave; and nevertheless, being Christians, they believed that they had only one human life to enjoy in this world. But Shinzaburō was a Buddhist, — with a million lives behind him and a million lives before him; and he was too selfish to give up even one miserable existence for the sake of the girl that came back to him from the dead. Then he was even more cowardly than selfish. Although a samurai by birth and training, he had to beg a priest to save him from ghosts. In every way he proved himself contemptible; and O-Tsuyu did quite right in choking him to death."

"From the Japanese point of view, likewise," my friend responded, " Shinzaburō is rather contemptible. But the use of this weak character helped the author to develop incidents that could not otherwise, perhaps, have been so effectively managed. To my thinking, the only attractive character in the story is that of O-Yoné : type of the old-time loyal and loving servant, — intelligent, shrewd, full of resource, — faithful not only unto death, but beyond death. . . . Well, let us go to Shin-Banzui-In."

We found the temple uninteresting, and the cemetery an abomination of desolation. Spaces once occupied by graves had been turned into potato-patches. Between were tombs leaning at all angles out of the perpendicular, tablets made illegible by scurf, empty pedestals, shattered water-tanks, and statues of Buddhas without heads or hands. Recent rains had soaked the black soil, — leaving here and there small pools of slime about

which swarms of tiny frogs were hopping. Everything — excepting the potato-patches — seemed
to have been neglected for years. In a shed just
within the gate, we observed a woman cooking ;
and my companion presumed to ask her if she
knew anything about the tombs described in the
Romance of the Peony-Lantern.

"Ah! the tombs of O-Tsuyu and O-Yoné ? "
she responded, smiling ; — " you will find them
near the end of the first row at the back of the
temple — next to the statue of Jizō."

Surprises of this kind I had met with elsewhere
in Japan.

We picked our way between the rain-pools and
between the green ridges of young potatoes, —
whose roots were doubtless feeding on the substance of many another O-Tsuyu and O-Yoné ;
— and we reached at last two lichen-eaten tombs
of which the inscriptions seemed almost obliterated.
Beside the larger tomb was a statue of Jizō, with
a broken nose.

"The characters are not easy to make out,"
said my friend — " but wait ! " . . . He drew from
his sleeve a sheet of soft white paper, laid it over
the inscription, and began to rub the paper with a
lump of clay. As he did so, the characters appeared in white on the blackened surface.

" '*Eleventh day, third month — Rat, Elder Brother, Fire — Sixth year of Horéki* [A. D. 1756].' . . . This would seem to be the grave of some innkeeper of Nedzu, named Kichibei. Let us see what is on the other monument."

With a fresh sheet of paper he presently brought out the text of a kaimyō, and read, —

" '*En-myō-In, Hō-yō-I-tei-ken-shi, Hō-ni*' : — '*Nun-of-the-Law, Illustrious, Pure-of-heart-and-will, Famed-in-the-Law, — inhabiting the Mansion-of-the-Preaching-of-Wonder.*' . . . The grave of some Buddhist nun."

" What utter humbug ! " I exclaimed. " That woman was only making fun of us."

" Now," my friend protested, " you are unjust to the woman ! You came here because you wanted a sensation ; and she tried her very best to please you. You did not suppose that ghost-story was true, did you ? "

Footprints of the Buddha

Footprints of the Buddha

I WAS recently surprised to find, in Anderson's catalogue of Japanese and Chinese paintings in the British Museum, this remarkable statement: — "It is to be noted that in Japan the figure of the Buddha is never represented by the feet, or pedestal alone, as in the Amravâtî remains, and many other Indian art-relics." As a matter of fact the representation is not even rare in Japan. It is to be found not only upon stone monuments, but also in religious paintings, — especially certain kakémono suspended in temples. These kakémono usually display the footprints upon a very large scale, with a multitude of mystical symbols and characters. The sculptures may be less common; but in Tōkyō alone there are a number of *Butsu-sohu-séki*, or "Buddha-foot stones," which I have seen, — and probably several which I have not seen. There is one at the temple of Ekō-In, near Ryōgoku-bashi; one at the temple of Dentsu-In, in Koishikawa; one at the temple of Denbō-In, in Asakusa; and a beautiful example at Zōjōji in Shiba. These are not cut out of a single block, but are composed of fragments cemented into the irregular traditional shape, and capped with a heavy slab of Nebukawa granite, on the polished surface of which the design is engraved in lines about one-tenth of an inch in depth. I should judge the average height of these pedestals to be about two feet four inches, and their greatest diameter about three feet. Around the footprints there are carved (in most of the examples) twelve little bunches of leaves and buds of the *Bodai-jū* (" Bodhidruma "), or Bodhi-tree of Buddhist legend. In all cases the footprint design is about the same; but the monuments are different in quality and finish. That of Zōjōji, — with figures of divinities cut in low relief on its sides, — is the most ornate and costly of the four. The specimen at Ekō-In is very poor and plain.

The first *Butsu-soku-sèki* made in Japan was that erected at Tōdaiji, in Nara. It was designed after a similar monument in China, said to be the faithful copy of an Indian original. Concerning this Indian original, the following tradition is given in an old Buddhist book [1] : — " In a temple of the province of Makada [*Maghada*] there is a great stone. The Buddha once trod upon this stone; and the prints of the soles of his feet remain upon its surface. The length of the impressions is one foot and eight inches,[2] and the width of them a little more than six inches. On the sole-part of each footprint there is the impression of a wheel; and upon each of the prints of the ten toes there is a flower-like design, which sometimes radiates light. When the Buddha felt that the time of his Nirvana was approaching, he went to Kushina [*Kusinârâ*], and there stood upon that stone. He stood with his face to the south.   Then he said to his disciple Anan [*Ananda*] : — ' In this place I leave the impression of my feet, to remain for a last

---

[1] The Chinese title is pronounced by Japanese as *Sei-iki-ki*. "Sei-Iki" (the Country of the West) was the old Japanese name for India; and thus the title might be rendered, " The Book about India." I suppose this is the work known to Western scholors as *Si-yu-ki*.

[2] " One *shaku* and eight *sun*." But the Japanese foot and inch are considerably longer than the English.

token. Although a king of this country will try to destroy the impression, it can never be entirely destroyed.' And indeed it has not been destroyed unto this day. Once a king who hated Buddhism caused the top of the stone to be pared off, so as to remove the impression; but after the surface had been removed, the footprints reappeared upon the stone."

Concerning the virtue of the representation of the footprints of the Buddha, there is sometimes quoted a text from the *Kwan-butsu-sanmai-kyō* ["Buddha-dhyâna-samâdhi-sâgara-sûtra"], thus translated for me: — "In that time Shaka ["Sâkyamuni"] lifted up his foot. . . . When the Buddha lifted up his foot all could perceive upon the sole of it the appearance of a wheel of a thousand spokes. . . . And Shaka said: — 'Whosoever beholds the sign upon the sole of my foot shall be purified from all his faults. Even he who beholds the sign after my death shall be delivered from all the evil results of all his errors.'" Various other texts of Japanese Buddhism affirm that whoever looks upon the footprints of the Buddha "shall be freed from the bonds of error, and conducted upon the Way of Enlightenment."

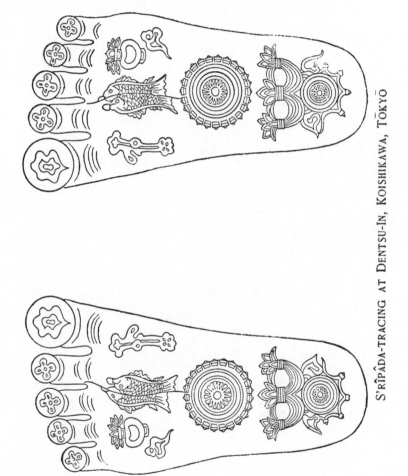

S'RÎPÂDA-TRACING AT DENTSU-IN, KOISHIKAWA, TŌKYŌ

An outline of the footprints as engraved on one of the Japanese pedestals[1] should have some interest even for persons familiar with Indian sculptures of the S'rîpâda. The double-page drawing, accompanying this paper, and showing both footprints, has been made after the tracing at Dentsu-In, where the footprints have the full legendary dimension. It will be observed that there are only seven emblems: these are called in Japan the *Shichi-Sō*, or "Seven Appearances." I got some information about them from the *Shō-Ekō-Hō-Kwan*, — a book used by the Jōdo sect. This book also contains rough woodcuts of the footprints; and one of them I reproduce here for the purpose of calling attention to the curious form of the emblems upon the toes. They are said to be modifications of the *manji*, or svastika (卍); but I doubt it. In the *Butsu-soku-séki*-tracings, the corresponding figures suggest the "flower-like design" mentioned in the tradition of the Maghada stone; while the symbols in the book-print suggest fire. Indeed their outline so much

---

[1] A monument at Nara exhibits the *S'rîpâda* in a form differing considerably from the design upon the Tōkyō pedestals.

resembles the conventional flamelet-design of Buddhist decoration, that I cannot help thinking them originally intended to indicate the traditional luminosity of the footprints. Moreover,

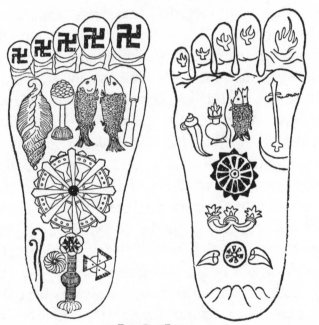

釋尊足下千輻輪相圖

SHŌ-EKŌ-HŌ-KWAN

there is a text in the book called *Hō-Kai-Shidai* that lends support to this supposition: — "The sole of the foot of the Buddha is flat, — like the base of a toilet-stand. . . . Upon it are lines forming the appearance of a wheel of a thousand spokes. . . . The toes are slender, round, long, straight, graceful, *and somewhat luminous.*"

The explanation of the Seven Appearances which is given by the *Shō-Ekō-Hō-Kwan* cannot be called satisfactory; but it is not without interest in relation to Japanese popular Buddhism. The emblems are considered in the following order : —

I. — *The Svastikâ.*   The figure upon each toe is said to be a modification of the *manji* [1] (卍) ; and although I doubt whether this is always the case, I have observed that on some of the large kakémono representing the footprints, the emblem really *is* the svastikâ, — not a flamelet nor a flower-shape.[2]   The Japanese commentator explains the svastikâ as a symbol of " everlasting bliss."

II. — *The Fish (Gyo).*   The fish signifies freedom from all restraints.   As in the water a fish moves easily in any direction, so in the Buddha-state the fully-emancipated knows no restraints or obstructions.

---

[1] Lit.: " The thousand-character " sign.

[2] On some monuments and drawings there is a sort of disk made by a single line in spiral, on each toe, — together with the image of a small wheel.

III. — *The Diamond-Mace* (Jap. *Kongō-sho ;* — Sansc. " Vadjra "). Explained as signifying the divine force that " strikes and breaks all the lusts (*bonnō*) of the world."

IV. — *The Conch-Shell* (Jap. " *Hora* ") *or Trumpet*. Emblem of the preaching of the Law. The book *Shin-ʐoku-butsu-ji-hen* calls it the symbol of the voice of the Buddha. The *Dai-hi-kyō* calls it the token of the preaching and of the power of the Mâhâyâna doctrine. The *Dai-Nichi-Kyō* says : — " At the sound of the blowing of the shell, all the heavenly deities are filled with delight, and come to hear the Law."

V. — *The Flower-Vase* (Jap. " *Hanagamé* "). Emblem of *murō*, — a mystical word which might be literally rendered as " not-leaking," — signifying that condition of supreme intelligence triumphant over birth and death.

VI. — *The Wheel-of-a-Thousand-Spokes* (Sansc. " Tchakra "). This emblem, called in Japanese *Senfuku-rin-sō*, is curiously explained by various quotations. The *Hokké-Monku* says : — " The effect of a wheel is to crush something ; and the effect of the Buddha's preaching is to crush all delusions, errors, doubts, and superstitions. Therefore preaching the doctrine is called, 'turning the Wheel.' " . . . The *Sei-Ri-Ron* says: " Even as the common wheel has its spokes and its hub, so in Buddhism there are many branches of the *Hasshi Shōdo* ('Eight-fold Path,' or eight rules of conduct)."

VII. — *The Crown of Brahmâ.* Under the heel of the Buddha is the Treasure-Crown (*Hō-Kwan*) of Brahmâ (*Bon-Ten-O*), — in symbol of the Buddha's supremacy above the gods.

But I think that the inscriptions upon any of these *Butsu-soku-séki* will be found of more significance than the above imperfect attempts at an explanation of the emblems. The inscriptions upon the monument at Dentsu-In are typical. On different sides of the structure, — near the top, and placed by rule so as to face certain points of the compass, — there are engraved five Sanscrit characters which are symbols of the Five Elemental Buddhas, together with scriptural and commemorative texts. These latter have been translated for me as follows: —

The HO-KO-HON-NYO-KYO *says : — " In that time, from beneath his feet, the Buddha radiated a light having the appearance of a wheel of a thousand spokes. And all who saw that radiance became strictly upright, and obtained the Supreme Enlightenment."*

The KWAN-BUTSU-SANMAI-KYO *says : —" Whosoever looks upon the footprints of the Buddha shall be freed from the results even of innumerable thousands of imperfections."*

The BUTSU-SETSU-MU-RYO-JU-KYO *says : — " In the land that the Buddha threads in journeying, there is not even one person in all the multitude of the villages who is not benefited. Then throughout the world there is peace and good will. The sun and the moon shine clear and bright. Wind and rain come only at a suitable time. Calamity and pestilence cease. The country prospers ; the people are free from care. Weapons become useless. All men reverence religion, and regulate their conduct in all matters with earnestness and modesty."*

[*Commemorative Text.*]

— The Fifth Month of the Eighteenth Year of Meiji, all the priests of this temple made and set up this pedestal-stone, bearing the likeness of the footprints of the Buddha, and placed the same within the main court of Dentsu-In, in order that the seed of holy enlightenment might be sown for future time, and for the sake of the advancement of Buddhism.

TAIJO, priest, — being the sixty-sixth chief-priest by succession of this temple, — has respectfully composed.

JUNYU, the minor priest, has reverentially inscribed.

II

Strange facts crowd into memory as one contemplates those graven footprints, — footprints giant-seeming, yet less so than the human personality of which they remain the symbol. Twenty-four hundred years ago, out of solitary meditation upon the pain and the mystery of being, the mind of an Indian pilgrim brought forth the highest truth ever taught to men, and in an era barren of science anticipated the uttermost knowledge of our present evolutional philosophy regarding the secret unity of life, the endless illusions of matter and of mind, and the birth and death of universes. He, by pure reason, — and he alone before our time, — found answers of worth to the questions of the Whence, the Whither, and the Why; — and he made with these answers another and a nobler faith than the creed of his fathers. He spoke, and returned to his dust; and the people worshipped the prints of his dead feet, because of the love that he had taught them. Thereafter waxed and waned the name of Alexander, and the power of Rome, and the might of Islam; — nations arose and vanished; — cities grew and were not; — the children of another civilization, vaster than Rome's, begirdled the earth with conquest, and founded far-off empires, and came at last to rule in the land of that pilgrim's birth. And these, rich in the wisdom of four and twenty centuries, wondered at the beauty of his message, and caused all that he had said and done to be written down anew in languages unborn at the time when he lived and taught. Still burn his footprints in the East; and still the great West, marvelling, follows their gleam to seek the Supreme Enlightenment. Even thus, of old, Milinda the king followed the way to the house of Nagasena, — at first only to question, after the subtle method of the Greeks; yet, later, to accept with noble reverence the nobler method of the Master.

Ululation

Ululation

SHE is lean as a wolf, and very old, — the white bitch that guards my gate at night. She played with most of the young men and women of the neighborhood when they were boys and girls. I found her in charge of my present dwelling on the day that I came to occupy it. She had guarded the place, I was told, for a long succession of prior tenants — apparently with no better reason than that she had been born in the woodshed at the back of the house. Whether well or ill treated she had served all occupants faultlessly as a watch. The question of food as wages had never seriously troubled her, because most of the families of the street daily contributed to her support.

She is gentle and silent, — silent at least by day; and in spite of her gaunt ugliness, her pointed ears, and her somewhat unpleasant eyes, everybody is fond of her. Children ride on her back, and tease her at will; but although she has been known to make strange men feel uncomfortable, she never growls at a child. The reward of her patient good-nature is the friendship of the community. When the dog-killers come on their bi-annual round, the neighbors look after her interests. Once she was on the very point of being officially executed when the wife of the smith ran to the rescue, and pleaded successfully with the policeman superintending the massacres. "Put somebody's name on the dog," said the latter: "then it will be safe. Whose dog is it?" That question proved hard to answer. The dog was everybody's and nobody's — welcome everywhere but owned nowhere. "But where does it stay?" asked the puzzled constable. "It stays," said the smith's wife, "in the house of the foreigner." "Then let the foreigner's name be put upon the dog," suggested the policeman.

Accordingly I had my name painted on her back in big Japanese characters. But the neighbors did not think that she was sufficiently safeguarded by a single name. So the priest of Kobudera painted the name of the temple on her left side, in beautiful Chinese text; and the smith put the name of his shop on her right side; and

the vegetable-seller put on her breast the ideo-
graphs for " eight-hundred," — which represent
the customary abbreviation of the word *yaoya*
(vegetable-seller), — any yaoya being supposed
to sell eight hundred or more different things.
Consequently she is now a very curious-look-
ing dog ; but she is well protected by all that
calligraphy.

I have only one fault to find with her : she
howls at night. Howling is one of the few
pathetic pleasures of her existence. At first I
tried to frighten her out of the habit ; but finding that she refused to take me seriously, I concluded to let her howl. It would have been
monstrous to beat her.

Yet I detest her howl. It always gives me a
feeling of vague disquiet, like the uneasiness that
precedes the horror of nightmare. It makes
me afraid, — indefinably, superstitiously afraid.
Perhaps what I am writing will seem to you
absurd ; but you would not think it absurd if
you once heard her howl. She does not howl
like the common street-dogs. She belongs to
some ruder Northern breed, much more wolfish,
and retaining wild traits of a very peculiar kind.

And her howl is also peculiar. It is incomparably weirder than the howl of any European dog; and I fancy that it is incomparably older. It may represent the original primitive cry of her species, — totally unmodified by centuries of domestication.

It begins with a stifled moan, like the moan of a bad dream, — mounts into a long, long wail, like a wailing of wind, — sinks quavering into a chuckle, — rises again to a wail, very much higher and wilder than before, — breaks suddenly into a kind of atrocious laughter, — and finally sobs itself out in a plaint like the crying of a little child. The ghastliness of the performance is chiefly — though not entirely — in the goblin mockery of the laughing tones as contrasted with the piteous agony of the wailing ones: an incongruity that makes you think of madness. And I imagine a corresponding incongruity in the soul of the creature. I know that she loves me, — that she would throw away her poor life for me at an instant's notice. I am sure that she would grieve if I were to die. But she would not think about the matter like other dogs, — like a dog with hanging ears, for example. She is too savagely close to Nature for that. Were she to find herself alone with my corpse in some desolate place, she would first mourn wildly for her friend ; but, this duty performed, she would proceed to ease her sorrow in the simplest way possible, — by eating him, — by cracking his bones between those long wolf's-teeth of hers. And thereafter, with spotless conscience, she would sit down and utter to the moon the funeral cry of her ancestors.

It fills me, that cry, with a strange curiosity not less than with a strange horror, — because of certain extraordinary vowellings in it which always recur in the same order of sequence, and must represent particular forms of animal speech, — particular ideas. The whole thing is a song, — a song of emotions and thoughts not human, and therefore humanly unimaginable. But other dogs know what it means, and make answer over the miles of the night, — sometimes from so far away that only by straining my hearing to the uttermost can I detect the faint response. The words — (if I may call them words) — are very few ; yet, to judge by their emotional effect, they must signify a great deal. Possibly they mean things myriads of years old, — things relating to odors, to exhalations, to influences and effluences inapprehensible by duller human sense, — impulses also, impulses without name, bestirred in ghosts of dogs by the light of great moons.

Could we know the sensations of a dog, — the emotions and the ideas of a dog, we might discover some strange correspondence between their character and the character of that peculiar disquiet which the howl of the creature evokes. But since the senses of a dog are totally unlike those of a man, we shall never really know. And we can only surmise, in the vaguest way, the meaning of the uneasiness in ourselves. Some notes in the long cry, — and the weirdest of them, — oddly resemble those tones of the human voice that tell of agony and terror. Again, we have reason to believe that the sound of the cry itself became associated in human imagination, at some period enormously remote, with particular impressions of fear. It is a remarkable fact that in almost all countries (including Japan) the howling of dogs has been attributed to their perception of things viewless to man, and awful, — especially gods and ghosts; — and this unanimity of superstitious belief suggests that one element of the disquiet inspired by the cry is the dread of the supernatural. To-day we have ceased to be consciously afraid of the unseen ; — knowing that we ourselves are supernatural, — that even the physical man, with all his life of sense, is more ghostly than any ghost of old imagining : but some dim inheritance of the primitive fear still slumbers in our being, and wakens perhaps, like an echo, to the sound of that wail in the night.

Whatever thing invisible to human eyes the senses of a dog may betimes perceive, it can be nothing resembling our idea of a ghost. Most probably the mysterious cause of start and whine is not anything *seen*. There is no anatomical reason for supposing a dog to possess exceptional powers of vision. But a dog's organs of scent proclaim a faculty immeasurably superior to the sense of smell in man. The old universal belief in the superhuman perceptivities of the creature was a belief justified by fact ; but the perceptivities are not visual. Were the howl of a dog really — as once supposed — an outcry of ghostly terror, the meaning might possibly be, " *I smell Them !* " — but not, " *I see Them !* " No evidence exists to support the fancy that a dog can see any forms of being which a man cannot see.

But the night-howl of the white creature in my close forces me to wonder whether she does not *mentally* see something really terrible, — something which we vainly try to keep out of moral consciousness: the ghoulish law of life. Nay, there are times when her cry seems to me not the mere cry of a dog, but the voice of the law itself, — the very speech of that Nature so inexplicably called by poets the loving, the merciful, the divine! Divine, perhaps, in some unknowable ultimate way, — but certainly not merciful, and still more certainly not loving. Only by eating each other do beings exist! Beautiful to the poet's vision our world may seem, — with its loves, its hopes, its memories, its aspirations; but there is nothing beautiful in the fact that life is fed by continual murder, — that the tenderest affection, the noblest enthusiasm, the purest idealism, must be nourished by the eating of flesh and the drinking of blood. All life, to sustain itself, must devour life. You may imagine yourself divine if you please, — but you have to obey that law. Be, if you will, a vegetarian: none the less you must eat forms that have feeling and desire. Sterilize your food; and digestion stops. You cannot even drink without swallowing life. Loathe

the name as we may, we are cannibals; — all being essentially is One; and whether we eat the flesh of a plant, a fish, a reptile, a bird, a mammal, or a man, the ultimate fact is the same. And for all life the end is the same: every creature, whether buried or burnt, is devoured, — and not only once or twice, — nor a hundred, nor a thousand, nor a myriad times! Consider the ground upon which we move, the soil out of which we came; — think of the vanished billions that have risen from it and crumbled back into its latency to feed what becomes our food! Perpetually we eat the dust of our race, — *the substance of our ancient selves*.

But even so-called inanimate matter is self-devouring. Substance preys upon substance. As in the droplet monad swallows monad, so in the vast of Space do spheres consume each other. Stars give being to worlds and devour them; planets assimilate their own moons. All is a ravening that never ends but to recommence. And unto whomsoever thinks about these matters, the story of a divine universe, made and ruled by paternal love, sounds less persuasive than the Polynesian tale that the souls of the dead are devoured by the gods.

Monstrous the law seems, because we have developed ideas and sentiments which are opposed to this demoniac Nature, — much as voluntary movement is opposed to the blind power of gravitation. But the possession of such ideas and sentiments does but aggravate the atrocity of our situation, without lessening in the least the gloom of the final problem.

Anyhow the faith of the Far East meets that problem better than the faith of the West. To the Buddhist the Cosmos is not divine at all — quite the reverse. It is Karma; — it is the creation of thoughts and acts of error; — it is not governed by any providence; — it is a ghastliness, a nightmare. Likewise it is an illusion. It seems real only for the same reason that the shapes and the pains of an evil dream seem real to the dreamer. Our life upon earth is a state of sleep. Yet we do not sleep utterly. There are gleams in our darkness, — faint auroral wakenings of Love and Pity and Sympathy and Magnanimity: these are selfless and true; — these are eternal and divine; — these are the Four Infinite Feelings in whose after-glow all forms and illusions will vanish, like mists in the light of the sun. But, except in so far as we wake to these feelings, we are dreamers indeed, — moaning unaided in darkness, — tortured by shadowy horror. All of us dream; none are fully awake; and many, who pass for the wise of the world, know even less of the truth than my dog that howls in the night.

Could she speak, my dog, I think that she might ask questions which no philosopher would be able to answer. For I believe that she is tormented by the pain of existence. Of course I do not mean that the riddle presents itself to her as it does to us, — nor that she can have reached any abstract conclusions by any mental processes like our own. The external world to her is " a continuum of smells." She thinks, compares, remembers, reasons by smells. By smell she makes her estimates of character: all her judgments are founded upon smells. Smelling thousands of things which we cannot smell at all, she must comprehend them in a way of which we can form no idea. Whatever she knows has been learned through mental operations of an utterly unimaginable kind. But we may be tolerably sure that she thinks about most things in some odor-relation to the experience of eating or to the intuitive dread of being eaten. Certainly she knows a great deal more about the earth on which we tread than would be good for us to know; and probably, if capable of speech, she could tell us the strangest stories of air and water. Gifted, or afflicted, as she is with such terribly penetrant power of sense, her notion of apparent realities must be worse than sepulchral. Small wonder if she howl at the moon that shines upon such a world!

And yet she is more awake, in the Buddhist meaning, than many of us. She possesses a rude moral code — inculcating loyalty, submission, gentleness, gratitude, and maternal love; together with various minor rules of conduct; —and this simple code she has always observed. By priests her state is termed a state of darkness of mind, because she cannot learn all that men should learn; but according to her light she has done well enough to merit some better condition in her next rebirth. So think the people who know her. When she dies they will give her an humble funeral, and have a sûtra recited on behalf of her spirit. The priest will let a grave be made for her somewhere in the temple-garden, and will place over it a little sotoba bearing the text, — *Nyo-ʒé chikushō hotsu Bodai-shin* [1]: "Even within such as this animal, the Knowledge Supreme will unfold at last."

[1] Lit., "the Bodhi-mind;" — that is to say, the Supreme Enlightenment, the intelligence of Buddhahood itself.

Bits of Poetry

Bits of Poetry

I

AMONG a people with whom poetry has been for centuries a universal fashion of emotional utterance, we should naturally suppose the common ideal of life to be a noble one. However poorly the upper classes of such a people might compare with those of other nations, we could scarcely doubt that its lower classes were morally and otherwise in advance of our own lower classes. And the Japanese actually present us with such a social phenomenon.

Poetry in Japan is universal as the air. It is felt by everybody. It is read by everybody. It is composed by almost everybody, — irrespective of class and condition. Nor is it thus ubiquitous in the mental atmosphere only : it is everywhere to be heard by the ear, *and seen by the eye !*

As for audible poetry, wherever there is working there is singing. The toil of the fields and the labor of the streets are performed to the rhythm of chanted verse; and song would seem to be an expression of the life of the people in about the same sense that it is an expression of the life of cicadæ. . . . As for visible poetry, it appears everywhere, written or graven, — in Chinese or in Japanese characters, — as a form of decoration. In thousands and thousands of dwellings, you might observe that the sliding-screens, separating rooms or closing alcoves, have Chinese or Japanese decorative texts upon them; — and these texts are poems. In houses of the better class there are usually a number of *gaku*, or suspended tablets to be seen, — each bearing, for all design, a beautifully written verse. But poems can be found upon almost any kind of domestic utensil, — for example upon braziers, iron kettles, vases, wooden trays, lacquer ware, porcelains, chopsticks of the finer sort, — even toothpicks! Poems are painted upon shop-signs, panels, screens, and fans. Poems are printed upon towels, draperies, curtains, kerchiefs, silk-linings, and women's crêpe-silk underwear. Poems are stamped or worked upon letter-paper, envelopes, purses, mirror-cases, travelling-bags. Poems are inlaid upon enamelled ware, cut upon bronzes, graven upon metal pipes, embroidered upon tobacco-pouches. It were a hopeless effort to enumerate a tithe of the articles decorated with poetical texts. Probably my readers know of those social gatherings at which it is the custom to compose verses, and to suspend the compositions to blossoming trees, — also of the Tanabata festival in honor of certain astral gods, when poems inscribed on strips of colored paper, and attached to thin bamboos, are to be seen even by the roadside, — all fluttering in the wind like so many tiny flags. . . . Perhaps you might find your way to some Japanese hamlet in which there are neither trees nor flowers, but never to any hamlet in which there is no visible poetry. You might wander, — as I have done, — into a settlement so poor that you could not obtain there, for love or money, even a cup of real tea ; but I do not believe that you could discover a settlement in which there is nobody capable of making a poem.

II

Recently while looking over a manuscript-collection of verses, — mostly short poems of an emotional or descriptive character, — it occurred to me that a selection from them might serve to illustrate certain Japanese qualities of sentiment, as well as some little-known Japanese theories of artistic expression, — and I ventured forthwith upon this essay. The poems, which had been collected for me by different persons at many different times and places, were chiefly of the kind written on particular occasions, and cast into forms more serried, if not also actually briefer, than anything in Western prosody. Probably few of my readers are aware of two curious facts relating to this order of composition. Both facts are exemplified in the history and in the texts of my collection, — though I cannot hope, in my renderings, to reproduce the original effect, whether of imagery or of feeling.

The first curious fact is that, from very ancient times, the writing of short poems has been practised in Japan even more as a moral duty than

as a mere literary art. The old ethical teaching
was somewhat like this: — "Are you very
angry? — do not say anything unkind, but compose a poem. Is your best-beloved dead? — do
not yield to useless grief, but try to calm your
mind by making a poem. Are you troubled
because you are about to die, leaving so many
things unfinished? — be brave, and write a poem
on death! Whatever injustice or misfortune
disturbs you, put aside your resentment or your
sorrow as soon as possible, and write a few lines
of sober and elegant verse for a moral exercise."
Accordingly, in the old days, every form of
trouble was encountered with a poem. Bereave-
ment, separation, disaster called forth verses in
lieu of plaints. The lady who preferred death
to loss of honor, composed a poem before pierc-
ing her throat. The samurai sentenced to die
by his own hand, wrote a poem before perform-
ing *hara-kiri*. Even in this less romantic era of
Meiji, young people resolved upon suicide are
wont to compose some verses before quitting the
world. Also it is still the good custom to write a
poem in time of ill-fortune. I have frequently
known poems to be written under the most trying circumstances of misery or suffering, — nay,

even upon a bed of death ; — and if the verses did not display any extraordinary talent, they at least afforded extraordinary proof of self-mastery under pain. . . . Surely this fact of composition as ethical practice has larger interest than all the treatises ever written about the rules of Japanese prosody.

The other curious fact is only a fact of æsthetic theory. The common art-principle of the class of poems under present consideration is identical with the common principle of Japanese pictorial illustration. By the use of a few chosen words the composer of a short poem endeavors to do exactly what the painter endeavors to do with a few strokes of the brush, — to evoke an image or a mood, — to revive a sensation or an emotion. And the accomplishment of this purpose, — by poet or by picture-maker, — depends altogether upon capacity to *suggest*, and only to suggest. A Japanese artist would be condemned for attempting elaboration of detail in a sketch intended to recreate the memory of some landscape seen through the blue haze of a spring morning, or under the great blond light of an autumn afternoon. Not only would he be false to the traditions of his art: he would necessarily defeat his own end thereby. In the same way a poet would be condemned for attempting any *completeness* of utterance in a very short poem: his object should be only to stir imagination without satisfying it. So the term *ittakkiri* — meaning "all gone," or "entirely vanished," in the sense of "all told," — is contemptuously applied to verses in which the verse-maker has uttered his whole thought; — praise being reserved for compositions that leave in the mind the thrilling of a something unsaid. Like the single stroke of a temple-bell, the perfect short poem should set murmuring and undulating, in the mind of the hearer, many a ghostly aftertone of long duration.

III

But for the same reason that Japanese short poems may be said to resemble Japanese pictures, a full comprehension of them requires an intimate knowledge of the life which they reflect. And this is especially true of the emotional class of such poems, — a literal translation of which, in the majority of cases, would signify almost nothing to the Western mind. Here, for example, is a little verse, pathetic enough to Japanese comprehension : —

> Chōchō ni ! . .
> Kyonen shishitaru
> Tsuma koishi !

Translated, this would appear to mean only, — " *Two butterflies ! . . . Last year my dear wife died !* " Unless you happen to know the pretty Japanese symbolism of the butterfly in relation to happy marriage, and the old custom of sending with the wedding-gift a large pair of paper-butterflies (*ochō-méchō*), the verse might well seem to be less than commonplace. Or take this recent composition, by a University student, which has been praised by good judges : —

> Furosato ni
> Fubo ari — mushi no
> Koë-goë ! [1]

—" *In my native place the old folks [or, my parents] are — clamor of insect-voices !* " . . .

[1] I must observe, however, that the praise was especially evoked by the use of the term *koë-goë* — (literally meaning " voice after voice " or a crying of many voices) ; — and the special value of the syllables here can be appreciated only by a Japanese poet.

The poet here is a country-lad. In unfamiliar
fields he listens to the great autumn chorus of
insects ; and the sound revives for him the memory of his far-off home and of his parents. . . .
But here is something incomparably more touching, — though in literal translation probably
more obscure, — than either of the preceding
specimens : —

> Mi ni shimiru
> Kazé ya !
> Shōji ni
> Yubi no ato !

— "*Oh, body-piercing wind ! — that work of
little fingers in the shōji !*" [1] . . . What does
this mean ? It means the sorrowing of a mother
for her dead child. *Shōji* is the name given to
those light white-paper screens which in a Japanese house serve both as windows and doors, —
admitting plenty of light, but concealing, like
frosted glass, the interior from outer observation,
and excluding the wind. Infants delight to break
these by poking their fingers through the soft
paper : then the wind blows through the holes.
In this case the wind blows very cold indeed, —
into the mother's very heart ; — for it comes

[1] More literally : — " body-through-pierce wind — ah !
— *shōji*-in the traces of [viz.: holes made by] fingers ! "

through the little holes that were made by the fingers of her dead child.

The impossibility of preserving the inner quality of such poems in a literal rendering, will now be obvious. Whatever I attempt in this direction must of necessity be *ittakkiri*; — for the unspoken has to be expressed; and what the Japanese poet is able to say in seventeen or twenty-one syllables may need in English more than double that number of words. But perhaps this fact will lend additional interest to the following atoms of emotional expression: —

A Mother's Remembrance

Sweet and clear in the night, the voice of a boy at study,
Reading out of a book. . . . I also once had a boy!

A Memory in Spring

She who, departing hence, left to the flowers of the plum-
tree,
Blooming beside our eaves, the charm of her youth and beauty
And maiden pureness of heart, to quicken their flush and
fragrance, —
Ah! where does she dwell to-day, our dear little vanished
sister?

Fancies of Another Faith

(1) I sought in the place of graves the tomb of my vanished
friend:
From ancient cedars above there rippled a wild dove's cry.

(2) *Perhaps a freak of the wind — yet perhaps a sign of re-
    membrance, —*
This fall of a single leaf on the water I pour for the dead.

(3) *I whispered a prayer at the grave: a butterfly rose and
    fluttered —*
Thy spirit, perhaps, dear friend! . . .

In a Cemetery at Night

*This light of the moon that plays on the water I pour for the
dead,*
Differs nothing at all from the moonlight of other years.

After Long Absence

*The garden that once I loved, and even the hedge of the gar-
den, —*
All is changed and strange: the moonlight only is faithful; —
The moon alone remembers the charm of the time gone by!

Moonlight on the Sea

*O vapory moon of spring! — would that one plunge into ocean
Could win me renewal of life as a part of thy light on the
waters!*

After Farewell

Whither now should I look ? — where is the place of parting ?
Boundaries all have vanished; — nothing tells of direction :
Only the waste of sea under the shining moon!

Happy Poverty

*Wafted into my room, the scent of the flowers of the plum-tree
Changes my broken window into a source of delight.*

AUTUMN FANCIES

(1) *Faded the clover now ; — sere and withered the grasses :
What dreams the matsumushi [1] in the desolate autumn-
fields ?*

(2) *Strangely sad, I thought, sounded the bell of evening ; —
Haply that tone proclaimed the night in which autumn dies !*

(3) *Viewing this autumn-moon, I dream of my native village
Under the same soft light, — and the shadows about my
home.*

IN TIME OF GRIEF, HEARING A SÉMI (CICADA)

*Only " I," " I," — the cry of the foolish sémi !
Any one knows that the world is void as its cast-off shell.*

ON THE CAST–OFF SHELL OF A SÉMI

*Only the pitiful husk ! . . . O poor singer of summer,
Wherefore thus consume all thy body in song ?*

SUBLIMITY OF INTELLECTUAL POWER

*The mind that, undimmed, absorbs the foul and the pure to-
gether —
Call it rather a sea one thousand fathoms deep ! [2]*

---

[1] A musical cricket — *calyptotryphus marmoratus.*

[2] This is quite novel in its way, — a product of the University : the original runs thus : —

> Nigoréru mo
> Suméru mo tomo ni
> Iruru koso
> Chi-hiro no umi no
> Kokoro nari-keré !

SHINTŌ REVERY

Mad waves devour the rocks : I ask myself in the darkness,
" Have I become a god ?"   Dim is the night and wild !

" Have I become a god ? " —that is to say, " Have
I died ? — am I only a ghost in this desolation ? "
The dead, becoming *kami* or gods, are thought to
haunt wild solitudes by preference.

IV

The poems above rendered are more than pictorial: they suggest something of emotion or sentiment.   But there are thousands of pictorial poems
that do not; and these would seem mere insipidi-
ties to a reader ignorant of their true purpose.
When you learn that some exquisite text of gold
means only, " *Evening-sunlight on the wings of
the water-fowl,*" — or, " *Now in my garden the
flowers bloom, and the butterflies dance,*" — then
your first interest in decorative poetry is apt to
wither away.   Yet these little texts have a very
real merit of their own, and an intimate relation
to Japanese æsthetic feeling and experience.   Like
the pictures upon screens and fans and cups, they

give pleasure by recalling impressions of nature, by reviving happy incidents of travel or pilgrimage, by evoking the memory of beautiful days. And when this plain fact is fully understood, the persistent attachment of modern Japanese poets — notwithstanding their University training — to the ancient poetical methods, will be found reasonable enough.

I need offer only a very few specimens of the purely pictorial poetry. The following — mere thumb-nail sketches in verse — are of recent date.

LONESOMENESS

Furu-dera ya :
Kané mono iwazu;
Sakura chiru.

— "*Old temple : bell voiceless ; cherry-flowers fall.*"

MORNING AWAKENING AFTER A NIGHT'S REST IN A TEMPLE

Yamadera no
Shichō akéyuku :
Taki no oto.

— "*In the mountain-temple the paper mosquito-curtain is lighted by the dawn : sound of water-fall.*"

WINTER–SCENE

Yuki no mura;
Niwatori naité;
Aké shiroshi.

— *" Snow-village ; — cocks crowing ; — white dawn."*

Let me conclude this gossip on poetry by citing from another group of verses — also pictorial, in a certain sense, but chiefly remarkable for ingenuity — two curiosities of impromptu. The first is old, and is attributed to the famous poetess Chiyo. Having been challenged to make a poem of seventeen syllables referring to a square, a triangle, and a circle, she is said to have immediately responded, —

Kaya no té wo
Hitotsu hazushité,
Tsuki-mi kana !

— *" Detaching one corner of the mosquito-net, lo ! I behold the moon ! "* The top of the mosquito-net, suspended by cords at each of its four corners, represents the square ; — letting down the net at one corner converts the square into a triangle ; — and the moon represents the circle.

The other curiosity is a recent impromptu effort to portray, in one verse of seventeen syllables, the last degree of devil-may-care-poverty, — perhaps

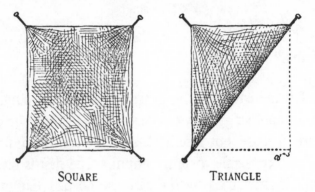

SQUARE   TRIANGLE

the brave misery of the wandering student; — and I very much doubt whether the effort could be improved upon : —

Nusundaru
Kagashi no kasa ni
Amé kyū nari.

— "*Heavily pours the rain on the hat that I stole from the scarecrow!*"

Japanese Buddhist Proverbs

Japanese Buddhist Proverbs

❧

A
S representing that general quality of moral experience which remains almost unaffected by social modifications of any sort, the proverbial sayings of a people must always possess a special psychological interest for thinkers. In this kind of folklore the oral and the written literature of Japan is rich to a degree that would require a large book to exemplify. To the subject as a whole no justice could be done within the limits of a single essay. But for certain classes of proverbs and proverbial phrases something can be done within even a few pages; and sayings related to Buddhism, either by allusion or derivation, form a class which seems to me particularly worthy of study. Accordingly, with the help of a Japanese friend, I have selected and translated the following series of examples, — choosing the more simple and

familiar where choice was possible, and placing the originals in alphabetical order to facilitate reference. Of course the selection is imperfectly representative; but it will serve to illustrate certain effects of Buddhist teaching upon popular thought and speech.

1. — *Akuji mi ni tomaru.*
All evil done clings to the body.[1]

2. — *Atama soru yori kokoro wo soré.*
Better to shave the heart than to shave the head.[2]

3. — *Au wa wakaré no hajimé.*
Meeting is only the beginning of separation.[3]

---

[1] The consequence of any evil act or thought never, — so long as karma endures, — will cease to act upon the existence of the person guilty of it.

[2] Buddhist nuns and priests have their heads completely shaven. The proverb signifies that it is better to correct the heart, — to conquer all vain regrets and desires, — than to become a religious. In common parlance the phrase "to shave the head" means to become a monk or a nun.

[3] Regret and desire are equally vain in this world of impermanency; for all joy is the beginning of an experience that must have its pain. This proverb refers directly to the sutra-text, — *Shōja hitsumetsu é-sha-jori,* — "All that live must surely die; and all that meet will surely part."

4. — *Banji wa yumé.*
All things [1] are merely dreams.

5. — *Bonbu mo satoréba hotoké nari.*
Even a common man by obtaining knowledge becomes a Buddha.[2]

6. — *Bonnō kunō.*
All lust is grief.[3]

7. — *Buppō to wara-ya no amé, dété kiké.*
One must go outside to hear Buddhist doctrine or the sound of rain on a straw roof.[4]

8. — *Busshō en yori okoru.*
Out of karma-relation even the divine nature itself grows.[5]

[1] Literally, " ten thousand things."

[2] The only real differences of condition are differences in knowledge of the highest truth.

[3] All sensual desire invariably brings sorrow.

[4] There is an allusion here to the condition of the *shukké* (priest): literally, " one who has left his house." The proverb suggests that the higher truths of Buddhism cannot be acquired by those who continue to live in the world of follies and desires.

[5] There is good as well as bad karma. Whatever happiness we enjoy is not less a consequence of the acts and thoughts of previous lives, than is any misfortune that

9. — *Enkō ga tsuki wo toran to suru ga gotoshi.*

Like monkeys trying to snatch the moon's reflection on water.[1]

10. — *En naki shujō wa doshi gatashi.*

To save folk having no karma-relation would be difficult indeed![2]

11. — *Fujō seppō suru hōshi wa, hirataké ni umaru.*

The priest who preaches foul doctrine shall be reborn as a fungus.

comes to us. Every good thought and act contributes to the evolution of the Buddha-nature within each of us. Another proverb [No. 10], — *En naki shujō wa doshi gatashi,* — further illustrates the meaning of this one.

[1] Allusion to a parable, said to have been related by the Buddha himself, about some monkeys who found a well under a tree, and mistook for reality the image of the moon in the water. They resolved to seize the bright apparition. One monkey suspended himself by the tail from a branch overhanging the well, a second monkey clung to the first, a third to the second, a fourth to the third, and so on, — till the long chain of bodies had almost reached the water. Suddenly the branch broke under the unaccustomed weight; and all the monkeys were drowned.

[2] No karma-relation would mean an utter absence of merit as well as of demerit.

12. — *Gaki mo ninʐu.*
Even gaki *(prêtas)* can make a crowd.[1]

13. — *Gaki no mé ni midʐu miéʐu.*
To the eyes of gaki water is viewless.[2]

14. — *Goshō wa daiji.*
The future life is the all-important thing.[3]

15. — *Gun-mō no tai-ʐō wo saguru ga gotoshi.*
Like a lot of blind men feeling a great elephant.[4]

---

[1] Literally: " Even gaki are a multitude (or, ' popula-
tion ')." This is a popular saying used in a variety of
ways. The ordinary meaning is to the effect that no matter
how poor or miserable the individuals composing a multitude, they collectively represent a respectable force.
Jocosely the saying is sometimes used of a crowd of
wretched or tired-looking people, — sometimes of an assembly of weak boys desiring to make some demonstra-
tion, — sometimes of a miserable-looking company of
soldiers. — Among the lowest classes of the people it is
not uncommon to call a deformed or greedy person a
" gaki."

[2] Some authorities state that those *prêtas* who suffer
especially from thirst, as a consequence of faults committed
in former lives, are unable to see water. — This proverb is
used in speaking of persons too stupid or vicious to perceive a moral truth.

[3] The common people often use the curious expression
" *gosho-daiji* " as an equivalent for " extremely important."

[4] Said of those who ignorantly criticise the doctrines of

16. — *Gwai-men nyo-Bosatsu ; nai shin nyo-Yasha.*

In outward aspect a Bodhisattva ; at innermost heart a demon.[1]

17. — *Hana wa né ni kaeru.*
The flower goes back to its root.[2]

18. — *Hibiki no koë ni oʒuru ga gotoshi.*
Even as the echo answers to the voice.[3]

19. — *Hito wo tasukéru ga shukké no yuku.*
The task of the priest is to save mankind.

Buddhism. — The proverb alludes to a celebrated fable in the *Avadânas*, about a number of blind men who tried to decide the form of an elephant by feeling the animal. One, feeling the leg, declared the elephant to be like a tree ; another, feeling the trunk only, declared the elephant to be like a serpent ; a third, who felt only the side, said that the elephant was like a wall ; a fourth, grasping the tail, said that the elephant was like a rope, etc.

[1] *Yasha* (Sanscrit *Yaksha*), a man-devouring demon.

[2] This proverb is most often used in reference to death, — signifying that all forms go back into the nothingness out of which they spring. But it may also be used in relation to the law of cause-and-effect.

[3] Referring to the doctrine of cause-and-effect. The philosophical beauty of the comparison will be appreciated only if we bear in mind that even the *tone* of the echo repeats the tone of the voice.

20. — *Hi wa kiyurédomo tō-shin wa kiyédʒu.*
Though the flame be put out, the wick remains.[1]

21. — *Hotoké mo motowa bonbu.*
Even the Buddha was originally but a common man.

22. — *Hotoké ni naru mo shami wo heru.*
Even to become a Buddha one must first become a novice.

23. — *Hotoké no kao mo sando.*
Even a Buddha's face, — only three times.[2]

24. — *Hotoké tanondé Jigoku é yuku.*
Praying to Buddha one goes to hell.[3]

25. — *Hotoké tsukutté tamashii irédʒu.*
Making a Buddha without putting in the soul.[4]

---

[1] Although the passions may be temporarily overcome, their sources remain.   A proverb of like meaning is, *Bonnō no inu oëdomo saraʒu:* "Though driven away, the Dog of Lust cannot be kept from coming back again."

[2] This is a short popular form of the longer proverb, *Hotoké no kao mo sando naʒuréba, hara wo tatsu:* "Stroke even the face of a Buddha three times, and his anger will be roused."

[3] The popular saying, *Oni no Nembutsu,* —"a devil's praying," — has a similar meaning.

[4] That is to say, making an image of the Buddha without giving it a soul.   This proverb is used in reference to

26. — *Ichi-ju no kagé, ichi-ga no nagaré, tashō no en.*

Even [the experience of] a single shadow or a single flowing of water, is [made by] the karma-relations of a former life.[1]

27. — *Ichi-mō shū-mō wo hiku.*
One blind man leads many blind men.[2]

28. — *Ingwa na ko.*
A karma-child.[8]

the conduct of those who undertake to do some work, and leave the most essential part of the work unfinished. It contains an allusion to the curious ceremony called *Kai-gen*, or " Eye-Opening." This *Kai-gen* is a kind of consecration, by virtue of which a newly-made image is supposed to become animated by the real presence of the divinity represented.

[1] Even so trifling an occurrence as that of resting with another person under the shadow of a tree, or drinking from the same spring with another person, is caused by the karma-relations of some previous existence.

[2] From the Buddhist work *Dai-chi-dō-ron.* — The reader will find a similar proverb in Rhys-David's " *Buddhist Suttas* " (Sacred Books of the East), p. 173, — together with a very curious parable, cited in a footnote, which an Indian commentator gives in explanation.

[8] A common saying among the lower classes in reference to an unfortunate or crippled child. Here the word *ingwa* is used especially in the retributive sense. It usually signifies evil karma; *kwahō* being the term used in speaking of meri-

29. — *Ingwa wa, kuruma no wa.*

Cause-and-effect is like a wheel.[1]

30. — *Innen ga fukai.*

The karma-relation is deep.[2]

31. — *Inochi wa fū-ʒen no tomoshibi.*

Life is a lamp-flame before a wind.[3]

32. — *Issun no mushi ni mo, gobu no tam-ashii.*

Even a worm an inch long has a soul half-an-inch long.[4]

torious karma and its results. While an unfortunate child is spoken of as "a child of *ingwa*," a very lucky person is called a "*kwahō-mono*," — that is to say, an instance, or example of *kwahō*.

[1] The comparison of *karma* to the wheel of a wagon will be familiar to students of Buddhism. The meaning of this proverb is identical with that of the *Dhammapada* verse: — "If a man speaks or acts with an evil thought, pain follows him as the wheel follows the foot of the ox that draws the carriage."

[2] A saying very commonly used in speaking of the attachment of lovers, or of the unfortunate results of any close relation between two persons.

[3] Or, "like the flame of a lamp exposed to the wind." A frequent expression in Buddhist literature is "the Wind of Death."

[4] Literally, "has a soul of five *bu*," — five *bu* being equal to half of the Japanese inch. Buddhism forbids all taking

33. — Iwashi [1] *no atama mo shinjin kara.*

Even the head of an *iwashi*, by virtue of faith, [will have power to save, or heal].

34. — Jigō-jitoku. [2]

The fruit of one's own deeds [*in a previous state of existence*].

35. — Jigoku dé hotoké.

Like meeting with a Buddha in hell. [3]

of life, and classes as *living* things (*Ujō*) all forms having sentiency. The proverb, however, — as the use of the word "soul" (*tamashii*) implies, — reflects popular belief rather than Buddhist philosophy. It signifies that any life, however small or mean, is entitled to mercy.

[1] The *iwashi* is a very small fish, much resembling a sardine. The proverb implies that the object of worship signifies little, so long as the prayer is made with perfect faith and pure intention.

[2] Few popular Buddhist phrases are more often used than this. *Jigō* signifies one's own acts or thoughts; *jitoku*, to bring upon oneself, — nearly always in the sense of misfortune, when the word is used in the Buddhist way. "Well, it is a matter of *Jigō-jitoku,*" people will observe on seeing a man being taken to prison; meaning, "He is reaping the consequence of his own faults."

[3] Refers to the joy of meeting a good friend in time of misfortune. The above is an abbreviation. The full proverb is, *Jigoku dé hotoké ni ōta yo da.*

36. — *Jigoku Gokuraku wa kokoro ni ari.*
Hell and Heaven are in the hearts of men.[1]

37. — *Jigoku mo sumika.*
Even Hell itself is a dwelling-place.[2]

38. — *Jigoku ni mo shiru hito.*
Even in hell old acquaintances are welcome.

39. — *Kagé no katachi ni shitagau gotoshi.*
Even as the shadow follows the shape.[3]

40. — *Kané wa Amida yori hikaru.*
Money shines even more brightly than Amida.[4]

---

[1] A proverb in perfect accord with the higher Buddhism.

[2] Meaning that even those obliged to live in hell must learn to accommodate themselves to the situation. One should always try to make the best of circumstances. A proverb of kindred signification is, *Sumeba, Miyako:* "Wheresover one's home is, that is the Capital [or, Imperial City]."

[3] Referring to the doctrine of cause-and-effect. Compare with verse 2 of the *Dhammapada.*

[4] Amitâbha, the Buddha of Immeasurable Light. His image in the temples is usually gilded from head to foot. — There are many other ironical proverbs about the power of wealth, — such as *Jigoku no sata mo kané shidai:* "Even the Judgments of Hell may be influenced by money."

Jizō

EMMA DAI-Ō

41.—*Karu-toki no Jizō-gao; nasu-toki no Emma-gao.*

Borrowing-time, the face of Jizō; repaying-time, the face of Emma.[1]

42.—*Kiité Gokuraku, mité Jigoku.*

Heard of only, it is Paradise; seen, it is Hell.[2]

43.—*Kōji mon wo idézu: akuji sen ri wo hashiru.*

Good actions go not outside of the gate: bad deeds travel a thousand *ri*.

44.—*Kokoro no koma ni tadzuna wo yuru-suna.*

Never let go the reins of the wild colt of the heart.

45.—*Kokoro no oni ga mi wo séméru.*

The body is tortured only by the demon of the heart.[3]

---

[1] Emma is the Chinese and Japanese Yama,—in Buddhism the Lord of Hell, and the Judge of the Dead. The proverb is best explained by the accompanying drawings, which will serve to give an idea of the commoner representations of both divinities.

[2] Rumor is never trustworthy.

[3] Or "mind." That is to say that we suffer only from the consequences of our own faults.—The demon-torturer in the Buddhist hell says to his victim:— "Blame not me!— I am only the creation of your own deeds and thoughts: you made me for this!"—Compare with No. 36.

46. — *Kokoro no shi to wa naré ; kokoro wo shi to sezaré.*

Be the teacher of your heart: do not allow your heart to become your teacher.

47. — *Kono yo wa kari no yado.*
This world is only a resting-place.[1]

48. — *Kori wo chiribamé ; midzu ni égaku.*
To inlay ice ; to paint upon water.[2]

49. —

> *Korokoro to*
> *Naku wa yamada no*
> *Hototogisu,*
> *Chichi nitéya aran,*
> *Haha nitéya aran.*

The bird that cries *korokoro* in the mountain rice-field I know to be a *hototogisu ;* — yet it may

---

[1] "This world is but a travellers' inn," would be an almost equally correct translation. *Yado* literally means a lodging, shelter, inn ; and the word is applied often to those wayside resting-houses at which Japanese travellers halt during a journey. *Kari* signifies temporary, transient, fleeting, — as in the common Buddhist saying, *Kono yo kari no yo :* "This world is a fleeting world." Even Heaven and Hell represent to the Buddhist only halting places upon the journey to Nirvâna.

[2] Refers to the vanity of selfish effort for some merely temporary end.

have been my father; it may have been my mother.[1]

50. — *Ko wa Sangai no kubikase.*

A child is a neck-shackle for the Three States of Existence.[2]

51. — *Kuchi wa waȥawai no kado.*

The mouth is the front-gate of all misfortune.[3]

---

[1] This verse-proverb is cited in the Buddhist work *Wōjō Yōshū*, with the following comment: — " Who knows whether the animal in the field, or the bird in the mountain-wood, has nòt been either his father or his mother in some former state of existence?" — The *hototogisu* is a kind of cuckoo.

[2] That is to say, The love of parents for their child may impede their spiritual progress — not only in this world, but through all their future states of being, — just as a *kubikasé*, or Japanese cangue, impedes the movements of the person upon whom it is placed. Parental affection, being the strongest of earthly attachments, is particularly apt to cause those whom it enslaves to commit wrongful acts in the hope of benefiting their offspring. — The term *Sangai* here signifies the three worlds of Desire, Form, and Form-lessness, — all the states of existence below Nirvâna. But the word is sometimes used to signify the Past, the Present, and the Future.

[3] That is to say, The chief cause of trouble is unguarded speech. The word *Kado* means always the *main* entrance to a residence.

52. — *Kwahō wa, nété maté.*

If you wish for good luck, sleep and wait.[1]

53. — *Makanu tané wa haénu.*

Nothing will grow, if the seed be not sown.[2]

54. — *Matéba, kanrō no hiyori.*

If you wait, ambrosial weather will come.[3]

55. — *Meidō no michi ni Ō wa nashi.*

There is no King on the Road of Death.[4]

56. — *Mekura hebi ni ojizu.*

The blind man does not fear the snake.[5]

---

[1] *Kwahō*, a purely Buddhist term, signifying good fortune as the result of good actions in a previous life, has come to mean in common parlance good fortune of any kind. The proverb is often used in a sense similar to that of the English saying: "Watched pot never boils." In a strictly Buddhist sense it would mean, "Do not be too eager for the reward of good deeds."

[2] Do not expect harvest, unless you sow the seed. Without earnest effort no merit can be gained.

[3] *Kanrō*, the sweet dew of Heaven, or *amrita*. All good things come to him who waits.

[4] Literally, "on the Road of Meidō." The *Meidō* is the Japanese Hades, — the dark under-world to which all the dead must journey.

[5] The ignorant and the vicious, not understanding the law of cause-and-effect, do not fear the certain results of their folly.

57. — *Mitsuréba, kakuru.*

Having waxed, wanes.[1]

58. — *Mon zen no kozō narawanu kyō wo yomu.*

The shop-boy in front of the temple-gate repeats the sûtra which he never learned.[2]

59. — *Mujō no kazé wa, toki erabazu.*

The Wind of Impermanency does not choose a time.[8]

[1] No sooner has the moon waxed full than it begins to wane. So the height of prosperity is also the beginning of fortune's decline.

[2] *Kozō* means "acolyte" as well as "shop-boy," "errand-boy," or "apprentice;" but in this case it refers to a boy employed in a shop situated near or before the gate of a Buddhist temple. By constantly hearing the sûtra chanted in the temple, the boy learns to repeat the words. A proverb of kindred meaning is, *Kangaku-In no suzumé wa, Mōgyū wo sayézuru:* "The sparrows of Kangaku-In [an ancient seat of learning] chirp the Mōgyū," — a Chinese text formerly taught to young students. The teaching of either proverb is excellently expressed by a third: — *Narau yori wa naréro:* "Rather than study [an art], get accustomed to it," — that is to say, "keep constantly in contact with it." Observation and practice are even better than study.

[8] Death and Change do not conform their ways to human expectation.

60. — *Neko mo Busshō ari.*

In even a cat the Buddha-nature exists.[1]

61. — *Nèta ma ga Gokuraku.*

The interval of sleep is Paradise.[2]

62. — *Nijiu-go Bosatsu mo soré-soré no yaku.*

Even each of the Twenty-five Bodhisattvas has his own particular duty to perform.

63. — *Nin mité, hō toké.*

[First] see the person, [then] preach the doctrine.[3]

64. — *Ninshin ukégataku Buppō aigatashi.*

It is not easy to be born among men, and to meet with [*the good fortune of hearing the doctrine of*] Buddhism.[4]

---

[1] Notwithstanding the legend that only the cat and the *mamushi* (a poisonous viper) failed to weep for the death of the Buddha.

[2] Only during sleep can we sometimes cease to know the sorrow and pain of this world.   (Compare with No. 83.)

[3] The teaching of Buddhist doctrine should always be adapted to the intelligence of the person to be instructed. There is another proverb of the same kind, — *Ki ni yorité, hō wo toké:* "According to the understanding [of the person to be taught], preach the Law."

[4] Popular Buddhism teaches that to be born in the

65. — *Oni mo jiu-hachi.*

Even a devil [is pretty] at eighteen.[1]

66. — *Oni mo mi, narétaru ga yoshi.*

Even a devil, when you become accustomed to the sight of him, may prove a pleasant acquaintance.

67. — *Oni ni kanabō.*

An iron club for a demon.[2]

world of mankind, and especially among a people professing Buddhism, is a very great privilege. However miserable human existence, it is at least a state in which some knowledge of divine truth may be obtained; whereas the beings in other and lower conditions of life are relatively incapable of spiritual progress.

[1] There are many curious sayings and proverbs about the *oni*, or Buddhist devil, — such as *Oni no mé ni mo namida*, "tears in even a devil's eyes;" — "*Oni no kakuran*, "devil's cholera" (said of the unexpected sickness of some very strong and healthy person), etc., etc. — The class of demons called *Oni*, properly belong to the Buddhist hells, where they act as torturers and jailers. They are not to be confounded with the *Ma*, *Yasha*, *Kijin*, and other classes of evil spirits. In Buddhist art they are represented as beings of enormous strength, with the heads of bulls and of horses. The bull-headed demons are called *Go-ʒu*; the horse-headed *Mé-ʒu*.

[2] Meaning that great power should be given only to the strong.

68.— *Oni no nyōbo ni kijin.*

A devil takes a goblin to wife.[1]

69. — *Onna no ké ni wa dai-ʒō mo tsunagaru.*

With one hair of a woman you can tether even a great elephant.

70.— *Onna wa Sangai ni iyé nashi.*

Women have no homes of their own in the Three States of Existence.

71. — *Oya no ingwa ga ko ni mukuü.*

The karma of the parents is visited upon the child.[2]

72. — *Rakkwa éda ni kaeraʒu.*

The fallen blossom never returns to the branch.[3]

---

[1] Meaning that a wicked man usually marries a wicked woman.

[2] Said of the parents of crippled or deformed children. But the popular idea here expressed is not altogether in accord with the teachings of the higher Buddhism.

[3] That which has been done never can be undone: the past cannot be recalled. — This proverb is an abbreviation of the longer Buddhist text: *Rakkwa éda ni kaeraʒu; ha-kyō futatabi terasaʒu*: " The fallen blossom never returns to the branch; the shattered mirror never again reflects."

73. — Raku wa ku no tané ; ku wa raku no tané.

Pleasure is the seed of pain ; pain is the seed of pleasure.

74. — Rokudō wa, mé no maë.

The Six Roads are right before your eyes.[1]

75. — Sangai mu-an.

There is no rest within the Three States of Existence.

76. — Sangai ni kaki nashi ; — Rokudō ni hotori nashi.

There is no fence to the Three States of Existence ; — there is no neighborhood to the Six Roads.[2]

---

[1] That is to say, Your future life depends upon your conduct in this life; and you are thus free to choose for yourself the place of your next birth.

[2] Within the Three States (Sangai), or universes, of Desire, Form, and Formlessness; and within the Six Worlds, or conditions of being, — *Jigokudō* (Hell), *Gakidō* (Pretas), *Chikushōdō* (Animal Life), *Shuradō* (World of Fighting and Slaughter), *Ningendō* (Mankind), *Tenjōdō* (Heavenly Spirits) — all existence is included. Beyond there is only Nirvâna. "There is no fence," "no neighborhood," — that is to say, no limit beyond which to escape, — no middle-path between any two of these states. We shall be reborn into

77. — *Sangé ni wa sannen no tsumi mo hōrobu.*
One confession effaces the sins of even three years.

78. — *Sannin yoréba, kugai.*
Where even three persons come together, there is a world of pain.[1]

79. — *San nin yoréba, Monjū no chié.*
Where three persons come together, there is the wisdom of *Monjū.*[2]

80. — *Shaka ni sekkyō.*
Preaching to Sâkyamuni.

81. — *Shami kara chōrō.*
To become an abbot one must begin as a novice.

some one of them according to our karma. — Compare with No. 74.

[1] *Kugai* (lit.: "bitter world") is a term often used to describe the life of a prostitute.

[2] Monjū Bosatsu [*Mañdjus'ri Bodhisattva*] figures in Japanese Buddhism as a special divinity of wisdom. — The proverb signifies that three heads are better than one. A saying of like meaning is, *Hiza to mo dankō :* "Consult even with your own knee;" that is to say, Despise no advice, no matter how humble the source of it.

82. — *Shindaréba, koso ikitaré.*

Only by reason of having died does one enter into life.[1]

83. — *Shiranu ga, hotoké; minu ga, Goku-raku.*

Not to know is to be a Buddha; not to see is Paradise.

84. — *Shōbo ni kidoku nashi.*

There is no miracle in true doctrine.[2]

85. — *Shō-chié wa Bodai no samatagé.*

A little wisdom is a stumbling-block on the way to Buddhahood.[3]

[1] I never hear this singular proverb without being reminded of a sentence in Huxley's famous essay, *On the Physical Basis of Life:*—"The living protoplasm not only ultimately dies and is resolved into its mineral and lifeless constituents, but is always dying, and, strange as the paradox may sound, *could not live unless it died.*"

[2] Nothing can happen except as a result of eternal and irrevocable law.

[3] *Bodai* is the same word as the Sanscrit *Bodhi*, signifying the supreme enlightenment, — the knowledge that leads to Buddhahood; but it is often used by Japanese Buddhists in the sense of divine bliss, or the Buddha-state itself.

86. — *Shōshi no kukai hetori nashi.*

There is no shore to the bitter Sea of Birth and Death.[1]

87. — *Sodé no furi-awasé mo tashō no en.*

Even the touching of sleeves in passing is caused by some relation in a former life.

88. — *Sun zen; shaku ma.*

An inch of virtue; a foot of demon.[2]

89. — *Tanoshimi wa kanashimi no motoi.*

All joy is the source of sorrow.

90. — *Tondé hi ni iru natsu no mushi.*

So the insects of summer fly to the flame.[8]

91. — *Tsuchi-botoké no midzu-asobi.*

Clay-Buddha's water-playing.[4]

---

[1] Or, "the Pain-Sea of Life and Death."

[2] *Ma* (Sanscrit, *Mârakâyikas*) is the name given to a particular class of spirits who tempt men to evil. But in Japanese folklore the *Ma* have a part much resembling that occupied in Western popular superstition by goblins and fairies.

[8] Said especially in reference to the result of sensual indulgence.

[4] That is to say, "As dangerous as for a clay Buddha to play with water." Children often amuse themselves by making little Buddhist images of mud, which melt into shapelessness, of course, if placed in water.

92. — *Tsuki ni murakumo, hana ni kaẓé.*
Cloud-wrack to the moon ; wind to flowers.[1]

93. — *Tsuyu no inochi.*
Human life is like the dew of morning.

94. — *U-ki wa, kokoro ni ari.*
Joy and sorrow exist only in the mind.

95. — *Uri no tsuru ni nasubi wa naranu.*
Egg-plants do not grow upon melon-vines.

96. — *Uso mo hōben.*
Even an untruth may serve as a device.[2]

97. — *Waga ya no hotoké tattoshi.*
My family ancestors were all excellent
Buddhas.[3]

[1] The beauty of the moon is obscured by masses of
clouds; the trees no sooner blossom than their flowers are
scattered by the wind.   All beauty is evanescent.

[2] That is, a pious device for effecting conversion.
Such a device is justified especially by the famous parable
of the third chapter of the *Saddharma Pundarîka.*

[3] Meaning that one most reveres the *hotoké* — the
spirits of the dead regarded as Buddhas — in one's own
household-shrine.   There is an ironical play upon the
word *hotoké*, which may mean either a dead person simply,
or a Buddha.   Perhaps the spirit of this proverb may be
better explained by the help of another: *Nigéta sakana ni*

98. — *Yuki no haté wa, Nehan.*

The end of snow is Nirvâna.[1]

99. — *Zen ni wa ʒen no mukui ; aku ni wa aku no mukui.*

Goodness [*or, virtue*] is the return for goodness; evil is the return for evil.[2]

100. — *Zensé no yakusoku-goto.*

Promised [*or, destined*] from a former birth.[3]

chisai wa nai ; shinda kodomo ni warui ko wa nai — "Fish that escaped was never small; child that died was never bad."

[1] This curious saying is the only one in my collection containing the word *Nehan* (Nırvâna), and is here inserted chiefly for that reason. The common people seldom speak of *Nehan*, and have little knowledge of those profound doctrines to which the term is related. The above phrase, as might be inferred, is not a popular expression: it is rather an artistic and poetical reference to the aspect of a landscape covered with snow to the horizon-line, — so that beyond the snow-circle there is only the great void of the sky.

[2] Not so commonplace a proverb as might appear at first sight; for it refers especially to the Buddhist belief that every kindness shown to us in this life is a return of kindness done to others in a former life, and that every wrong inflicted upon us is the reflex of some injustice which we committed in a previous birth.

[3] A very common saying, — often uttered as a comment upon the unhappiness of separation, upon sudden mis-

fortune, upon sudden death, etc. It is used especially in relation to *shinjū*, or lovers' suicide. Such suicide is popularly thought to be a result of cruelty in some previous state of being, or the consequence of having broken, in a former life, the mutual promise to become husband and wife.

Suggestion

Suggestion

❦

I HAD the privilege of meeting him in Tōkyō, where he was making a brief stay on his way to India ; — and we took a long walk together, and talked of Eastern religions, about which he knew incomparably more than I. Whatever I could tell him concerning local beliefs, he would comment upon in the most startling manner, — citing weird correspondences in some living cult of India, Burmah, or Ceylon. Then, all of a sudden, he turned the conversation into a totally unexpected direction.

"I have been thinking," he said, "about the constancy of the relative proportion of the sexes, and wondering whether Buddhist doctrine furnishes an explanation. For it seems to me that, under ordinary conditions of karma, human rebirth would necessarily proceed by a regular alternation."

" Do you mean," I asked, " that a man would be reborn as a woman, and a woman as a man ? "

" Yes," he replied, " because desire is creative, and the desire of either sex is towards the other."

" And how many men," I said, " would want to be reborn as women ? "

" Probably very few," he answered. " But the doctrine that desire is creative does not imply that the individual longing creates its own satisfaction, — quite the contrary. The true teaching is that the result of every selfish wish is in the nature of a penalty, and that what the wish creates must prove — to higher knowledge at least — the folly of wishing."

" There you are right," I said; " but I do not yet understand your theory."

" Well," he continued, " if the physical conditions of human rebirth are all determined by the karma of the will relating to physical conditions, then sex would be determined by the will in relation to sex. Now the will of either sex is towards the other. Above all things else, excepting life, man desires woman, and woman man. Each individual, moreover, independently of any personal relation, feels perpetually, you say, the influence of some inborn feminine or masculine ideal, which you call ' a ghostly reflex of countless attachments in countless past lives.' And the insatiable desire represented by this ideal would of itself suffice to create the masculine or the feminine body of the next existence."

" But most women," I observed, " would like to be reborn as men ; and the accomplishment of that wish would scarcely be in the nature of a penalty."

" Why not ? " he returned. " The happiness or unhappiness of the new existence would not be decided by sex alone : it would of necessity depend upon many conditions in combination."

" Your theory is interesting," I said ; — " but I do not know how far it could be made to accord with accepted doctrine. . . . And what of the person able, through knowledge and practice of the higher law, to remain superior to all weaknesses of sex ? "

" Such a one," he replied, " would be reborn neither as man nor as woman, — providing there were no pre-existent karma powerful enough to check or to weaken the results of the self-conquest."

" Reborn in some one of the heavens ? " I queried, — " by the Apparitional Birth ? "

"Not necessarily," he said. "Such a one might be reborn in a world of desire, — like this, — but neither as man only, nor as woman only."

"Reborn, then, in what form?" I asked.

"In that of a perfect being," he responded. "A man or a woman is scarcely more than half-a-being, — because in our present imperfect state either sex can be evolved only at the cost of the other. In the mental and the physical composition of every man, there is undeveloped woman; and in the composition of every woman there is undeveloped man. But a being complete would be both perfect man and perfect woman, possessing the highest faculties of both sexes, with the weaknesses of neither. Some humanity higher than our own, — in other worlds, — might be thus evolved."

"But you know," I observed, "that there are Buddhist texts, — in the *Saddharma Pundarîka*, for example, and in the *Vinayas*, — which forbid. . . ."

"Those texts," he interrupted, "refer to imperfect beings — less than man and less than woman: they could not refer to the condition that I have been supposing. . . . But, remember,

I am not preaching a doctrine;—I am only hazarding a theory."

" May I put your theory some day into print ? " I asked.

" Why, yes," he made answer,— " if you believe it worth thinking about."

And long afterwards I wrote it down thus, as fairly as I was able, from memory.

Ingwa-banashi

Ingwa-banashi [1]

❦

T HE daimyō's wife was dying, and knew that she was dying. She had not been able to leave her bed since the early autumn of the tenth Bunsei. It was now the fourth month of the twelfth Bunsei, — the year 1829 by Western counting; and the cherry-trees were blossoming. She thought of the cherry-trees in her garden, and of the gladness of spring. She thought of her children. She thought of her husband's various concubines, — especially the Lady Yukiko, nineteen years old.

[1] Lit., " a tale of *ingwa*." *Ingwa* is a Japanese Buddhist term for evil karma, or the evil consequence of faults committed in a former state of existence. Perhaps the curious title of the narrative is best explained by the Buddhist teaching that the dead have power to injure the living only in consequence of evil actions committed by their victims in some former life. Both title and narrative may be found in the collection of weird stories entitled *Hyaku-Monogatari*.

"My dear wife," said the daimyō, "you have suffered very much for three long years. We have done all that we could to get you well, — watching beside you night and day, praying for you, and often fasting for your sake. But in spite of our loving care, and in spite of the skill of our best physicians, it would now seem that the end of your life is not far off. Probably we shall sorrow more than you will sorrow because of your having to leave what the Buddha so truly termed 'this burning-house of the world.' I shall order to be performed — no matter what the cost — every religious rite that can serve you in regard to your next rebirth; and all of us will pray without ceasing for you, that you may not have to wander in the Black Space, but may quickly enter Paradise, and attain to Buddhahood."

He spoke with the utmost tenderness, caressing her the while. Then, with eyelids closed, she answered him in a voice thin as the voice of an insect: —

"I am grateful — most grateful — for your kind words. . . . Yes, it is true, as you say, that I have been sick for three long years, and that I have been treated with all possible care and affection. . . . Why, indeed, should I turn away from the one true Path at the very moment of my death? . . . Perhaps to think of worldly matters at such a time is not right; — but I have one last request to make, — only one. . . . Call here to me the Lady Yukiko; — you know that I love her like a sister. I want to speak to her about the affairs of this household."

Yukiko came at the summons of the lord, and, in obedience to a sign from him, knelt down beside the couch. The daimyō's wife opened her eyes, and looked at Yukiko, and spoke: —

" Ah, here is Yukiko! . . . I am so pleased to see you, Yukiko! . . . Come a little closer, — so that you can hear me well: I am not able to speak loud. . . . Yukiko, I am going to die. I hope that you will be faithful in all things to our dear lord; — for I want you to take my place when I am gone. . . . I hope that you will always be loved by him, — yes, even a hundred times more than I have been, — and that you will very soon be promoted to a higher rank, and become his honored wife. . . . And I beg of you always to cherish our dear lord: never allow another woman to rob you of his affection. . . . This is what I wanted to say to you, dear Yukiko. . . . Have you been able to understand ? "

" Oh, my dear Lady," protested Yukiko, " do not, I entreat you, say such strange things to me! You well know that I am of poor and mean condition: — how could I ever dare to aspire to become the wife of our lord ! "

" Nay, nay ! " returned the wife, huskily, — "this is not a time for words of ceremony: let us speak only the truth to each other. After my death, you will certainly be promoted to a higher place; and I now assure you again that I wish you to become the wife of our lord — yes, I wish this, Yukiko, even more than I wish to become a Buddha ! . . . Ah, I had almost forgotten ! — I want you to do something for me, Yukiko. You know that in the garden there is a *yaĕ-ʒakura*,[1] which was brought here, the year before last, from Mount Yoshino in Yamato. I have been told that it is now in full bloom ; — and I wanted so much to see it in flower ! In a little while I shall be dead ; — I must see that tree before I die. Now I wish you to carry me into the garden — at once, Yukiko, — so that I can see it. . . . Yes,

---

[1] *Yaĕ-ʒakura, yaĕ-no-sakura,* a variety of Japanese cherry-tree that bears double-blossoms.

upon your back, Yukiko;—take me upon your back. . . ."

While thus asking, her voice had gradually become clear and strong,—as if the intensity of the wish had given her new force: then she suddenly burst into tears. Yukiko knelt motionless, not knowing what to do; but the lord nodded assent.

"It is her last wish in this world," he said. "She always loved cherry-flowers; and I know that she wanted very much to see that Yamato-tree in blossom. Come, my dear Yukiko, let her have her will."

As a nurse turns her back to a child, that the child may cling to it, Yukiko offered her shoulders to the wife, and said:—

"Lady, I am ready: please tell me how I best can help you."

"Why, this way!"—responded the dying woman, lifting herself with an almost super-human effort by clinging to Yukiko's shoulders. But as she stood erect, she quickly slipped her thin hands down over the shoulders, under the robe, and clutched the breasts of the girl, and burst into a wicked laugh.

"I have my wish!" she cried — "I have my wish for the cherry-bloom,[1] — but not the cherry-bloom of the garden! . . . I could not die before I got my wish. Now I have it! — oh, what a delight!"

And with these words she fell forward upon the crouching girl, and died.

The attendants at once attempted to lift the body from Yukiko's shoulders, and to lay it upon the bed. But — strange to say! — this seemingly easy thing could not be done. The cold hands had attached themselves in some unaccountable way to the breasts of the girl, — appeared to have grown into the quick flesh. Yukiko became senseless with fear and pain.

Physicians were called. They could not understand what had taken place. By no ordinary methods could the hands of the dead woman be unfastened from the body of her victim; — they so clung that any effort to remove them brought blood. This was not because the fingers held:

---

[1] In Japanese poetry and proverbial phraseology, the physical beauty of a woman is compared to the cherry-flower; while feminine moral beauty is compared to the plum-flower.

it was because the flesh of the palms had united itself in some inexplicable manner to the flesh of the breasts!

At that time the most skilful physician in Yedo was a foreigner, — a Dutch surgeon. It was decided to summon him. After a careful examination he said that he could not understand the case, and that for the immediate relief of Yukiko there was nothing to be done except to cut the hands from the corpse. He declared that it would be dangerous to attempt to detach them from the breasts. His advice was accepted; and the hands were amputated at the wrists. But they remained clinging to the breasts; and there they soon darkened and dried up, — like the hands of a person long dead.

Yet this was only the beginning of the horror.

Withered and bloodless though they seemed, those hands were not dead. At intervals they would stir — stealthily, like great grey spiders. And nightly therafter, — beginning always at the Hour of the Ox,[1] — they would clutch and

[1] In ancient Japanese time, the Hour of the Ox was the special hour of ghosts. It began at 2 A.M., and lasted until 4 A.M. — for the old Japanese hour was double the length of the modern hour. The Hour of the Tiger began at 4 A.M.

compress and torture.   Only at the Hour of the Tiger the pain would cease.

Yukiko cut off her hair, and became a mendicant-nun, — taking the religious name of Dassetsu. She had an *ihai* (mortuary tablet) made, bearing the *kaimyō* of her dead mistress, — " *Myō-Kō-In-Den Chiẓan-Ryō-Fu Daishi* " ; — and this she carried about with her in all her wanderings ; and every day before it she humbly besought the dead for pardon, and performed a Buddhist service in order that the jealous spirit might find rest.   But the evil karma that had rendered such an affliction possible could not soon be exhausted.   Every night at the Hour of the Ox, the hands never failed to torture her, during more than seventeen years, — according to the testimony of those persons to whom she last told her story, when she stopped for one evening at the house of Noguchi Dengozayémon, in the village of Tanaka in the district of Kawachi in the province of Shimotsuké.   This was in the third year of Kōkwa (1846).   Thereafter nothing more was ever heard of her.

Story of a Tengu

Story of a Tengu [1]

🜚

I
N the days of the Emperor Go-Reizen, there
was a holy priest living in the temple of
Seito, on the mountain called Hiyei-Zan,
near Kyōto. One summer day this good priest,
after a visit to the city, was returning to his temple
by way of Kita-no-Ōji, when he saw some boys
ill-treating a kite. They had caught the bird in
a snare, and were beating it with sticks. " Oh,
the poor creature ! " compassionately exclaimed

[1] This story may be found in the curious old Japanese
book called *Jikkun-Shō*. The same legend has furnished the
subject of an interesting *Nō*-play, called *Dai-É* (" The Great
Picture ").

In Japanese popular art, the Tengu are commonly represented either as winged men with beak-shaped noses, or as
birds of prey. There are different kinds of Tengu ; but all
are supposed to be mountain-haunting spirits, capable of
assuming many forms, and occasionally appearing as crows,
vultures, or eagles. Buddhism appears to class the Tengu
among the Mârakâyikas.

the priest; — "why do you torment it so, children?" One of the boys made answer: — "We want to kill it to get the feathers." Moved by pity, the priest persuaded the boys to let him have the kite in exchange for a fan that he was carrying; and he set the bird free. It had not been seriously hurt, and was able to fly away.

Happy at having performed this Buddhist act of merit, the priest then resumed his walk. He had not proceeded very far when he saw a strange monk come out of a bamboo-grove by the road-side, and hasten towards him. The monk respectfully saluted him, and said: — "Sir, through your compassionate kindness my life has been saved; and I now desire to express my gratitude in a fitting manner." Astonished at hearing himself thus addressed, the priest replied: — "Really, I cannot remember to have ever seen you before: please tell me who you are." "It is not wonderful that you cannot recognize me in this form," returned the monk: "I am the kite that those cruel boys were tormenting at Kita-no-Ōji. You saved my life; and there is nothing in this world more precious than life. So I now wish to return your kindness in some way or

other.   If there be anything that you would like
to have, or to know, or to see, — anything that I
can do for you, in short, — please to tell me ; for
as I happen to possess, in a small degree, the Six
Supernatural Powers, I am able to gratify almost
any wish that you can express."   On hearing
these words, the priest knew that he was speaking
with a Tengu ; and he frankly made answer : —
" My friend, I have long ceased to care for the
things of this world : I am now seventy years of
age ; — neither fame nor pleasure has any attraction
for me.   I feel anxious only about my future
birth; but as that is a matter in which no one can
help me, it were useless to ask about it.   Really,
I can think of but one thing worth wishing for.
It has been my life-long regret that I was not in
India in the time of the Lord Buddha, and could
not attend the great assembly on the holy mountain Gridhrakûta.   Never a day passes in which
this regret does not come to me, in the hour of
morning or of evening prayer.   Ah, my friend !
if it were possible to conquer Time and Space,
like the Bodhisattvas, so that I could look upon that
marvellous assembly, how happy should I be ! "
— " Why," the Tengu exclaimed, " that pious
wish of yours can easily be satisfied.   I perfectly

well remember the assembly on the Vulture Peak ;
and I can cause everything that happened there to
reappear before you, exactly as it occurred.   It is
our greatest delight to represent such holy matters.
. . . Come this way with me ! "

And the priest suffered himself to be led to a
place among pines, on the slope of a hill.   " Now,"
said the Tengu, " you have only to wait here for
awhile, with your eyes shut.   Do not open them
until you hear the voice of the Buddha preaching
the Law.   Then you can look.   But when you
see the appearance of the Buddha, you must not
allow your devout feelings to influence you in any
way ; — you must not bow down, nor pray, nor
utter any such exclamation as, ' *Even so, Lord !* '
or ' *O thou Blessed One !* '   You must not speak
at all.   Should you make even the least sign
of reverence, something very unfortunate might
happen to me."   The priest gladly promised to
follow these injunctions ; and the Tengu hurried
away as if to prepare the spectacle.

The day waned and passed, and the darkness
came ; but the old priest waited patiently beneath
a tree, keeping his eyes closed.   At last a voice
suddenly resounded above him, — a wonderful

voice, deep and clear like the pealing of a mighty bell, — the voice of the Buddha Sâkyamuni proclaiming the Perfect Way. Then the priest, opening his eyes in a great radiance, perceived that all things had been changed: the place was indeed the Vulture Peak, — the holy Indian mountain Gridhrakûta; and the time was the time of the Sûtra of the Lotos of the Good Law. Now there were no pines about him, but strange shining trees made of the Seven Precious Substances, with foliage and fruit of gems; — and the ground was covered with Mandârava and Manjûshaka flowers showered from heaven; — and the night was filled with fragrance and splendour and the sweetness of the great Voice. And in mid-air, shining as a moon above the world, the priest beheld the Blessed One seated upon the Lion-throne, with Samantabhadra at his right hand, and Mañjusrî at his left, — and before them assembled — immeasurably spreading into Space, like a flood of stars — the hosts of the Mahâsattvas and the Bodhisattvas with their countlesss following: " gods, demons, Nâgas, goblins, men, and beings not human." Sâriputra he saw, and Kâsyapa, and Ânanda, with all the disciples of the Tathâgata, — and the Kings of the Devas, — and

the Kings of the Four Directions, like pillars of
fire, — and the great Dragon-Kings, — and the
Gandharvas and Garudas,— and the Gods of
the Sun and the Moon and the Wind, — and the
shining myriads of Brahma's heaven. And
incomparably further than even the measureless
circling of the glory of these, he saw — made
visible by a single ray of light that shot from the
forehead of the Blessed One to pierce beyond
uttermost Time — the eighteen hundred thousand
Buddha-fields of the Eastern Quarter with all
their habitants, — and the beings in each of the
Six States of Existence, — and even the shapes
of the Buddhas extinct, that had entered into
Nirvâna. These, and all the gods, and all the
demons, he saw bow down before the Lion-
throne ; and he heard that multitude incalculable
of beings praising the Sûtra of the Lotos of the
Good Law, — like the roar of a sea before the
Lord. Then forgetting utterly his pledge, — foolishly dreaming that he stood in the very presence
of the very Buddha, — he cast himself down in
worship with tears of love and thanksgiving ;
crying out with a loud voice, " *O thou Blessed
One !* " . . .

Instantly with a shock as of earthquake the

stupendous spectacle disappeared ; and the priest found himself alone in the dark, kneeling upon the grass of the mountain-side. Then a sadness unspeakable fell upon him, because of the loss of the vision, and because of the thoughtlessness that had caused him to break his word. As he sorrowfully turned his steps homeward, the goblin-monk once more appeared before him, and said to him in tones of reproach and pain : — " Because you did not keep the promise which you made to me, and heedlessly allowed your feelings to overcome you, the Gohōtendo, who is the Guardian of the Doctrine, swooped down suddenly from heaven upon us, and smote us in great anger, crying out, ' *How do ye dare thus to deceive a pious person ?* ' Then the other monks, whom I had assembled, all fled in fear. As for myself, one of my wings has been broken, — so that now I cannot fly." And with these words the Tengu vanished forever.

At Yaidzu

At Yaidzu

❦

I

UNDER a bright sun the old fishing-town of Yaidzu has a particular charm of neutral color. Lizard-like it takes the grey tints of the rude grey coast on which it rests, — curving along a little bay. It is sheltered from heavy seas by an extraordinary rampart of boulders. This rampart, on the water-side, is built in the form of terrace-steps; — the rounded stones of which it is composed being kept in position by a sort of basket-work woven between rows of stakes driven deeply into the ground, — a separate row of stakes sustaining each of the grades. Looking landward from the top of the structure, your gaze ranges over the whole town, — a broad space of grey-tiled roofs and weather-worn grey timbers, with here and there a pine-grove marking the place of a temple-court. Seaward, over leagues of water, there is a grand view, — a jagged blue range of peaks crowding sharply into the horizon, like prodigious amethysts, — and beyond them, to the left, the glorious spectre of Fuji, towering enormously above everything. Between sea-wall and sea there is no sand,— only a grey slope of stones, chiefly boulders; and these roll with the surf so that it is ugly work trying to pass the breakers on a rough day. If you once get struck by a stone-wave, — as I did several times, — you will not soon forget the experience.

At certain hours the greater part of this rough slope is occupied by ranks of strange-looking craft, — fishing-boats of a form peculiar to the locality. They are very large, — capable of carrying forty or fifty men each; — and they have queer high prows, to which Buddhist or Shintō charms (*mamori* or *shugo*) are usually attached. A common form of Shintō written charm (*shugo*) is furnished for this purpose from the temple of the Goddess of Fuji: the text reads : — *Fuji-san chōjō Sengen-gu dai-gyō manzoku*, — meaning that the owner of the boat pledges himself, in case of good-fortune at fishing, to perform great austerities in honor of the divinity whose shrine is upon the summit of Fuji.

In every coast-province of Japan, — and even at different fishing-settlements of the same province, — the forms of boats and fishing-implements are peculiar to the district or settlement. Indeed it will sometimes be found that settlements, within a few miles of each other, respectively manufacture nets or boats as dissimilar in type as might be the inventions of races living thousands of miles apart. This amazing variety may be in some degree due to respect for local tradition, — to the pious conservatism that preserves ancestral teaching and custom unchanged through hundreds of years: but it is better explained by the fact that different communities practise different kinds of fishing; and the shapes of the nets or the boats made, at any one place, are likely to prove, on investigation, the inventions of a special experience. The big Yaidzu boats illustrate this fact. They were devised according to the particular requirements of the Yaidzu-fishing-industry, which supplies dried *katsuo* (bonito) to all parts of the Empire; and it was necessary that they should be able to ride a very rough

sea. To get them in or out of the water is a
heavy job; but the whole village helps. A kind
of slipway is improvised in a moment by laying
flat wooden frames on the slope in a line; and
over these frames the flat-bottomed vessels are
hauled up or down by means of long ropes. You
will see a hundred or more persons thus engaged
in moving a single boat, — men, women, and
children pulling together, in time to a curious
melancholy chant. At the coming of a typhoon,
the boats are moved far back into the streets.
There is plenty of fun in helping at such work;
and if you are a stranger, the fisher-folk will
perhaps reward your pains by showing you the
wonders of their sea : crabs with legs of aston-
ishing length, balloon-fish that blow themselves
up in the most absurd manner, and various other
creatures of shapes so extraordinary that you can
scarcely believe them natural without touching
them.

The big boats with holy texts at their prows are
not the strangest objects on the beach. Even
more remarkable are the bait-baskets of split
bamboo, — baskets six feet high and eighteen
feet round, with one small hole in the dome-

shaped top. Ranged along the sea-wall to dry, they might at some distance be mistaken for habitations or huts of some sort. Then you see great wooden anchors, shaped like ploughshares, and shod with metal; iron anchors, with four flukes ; prodigious wooden mallets, used for driving stakes ; and various other implements, still more unfamiliar, of which you cannot even imagine the purpose. The indescribable antique queerness of everything gives you that weird sensation of remoteness, — of the far away in time and place, — which makes one doubt the reality of the visible. And the life of Yaidzu is certainly the life of many centuries ago. The people, too, are the people of Old Japan: frank and kindly as children — good children, — honest to a fault, innocent of the further world, loyal to the ancient traditions and the ancient gods.

II

I happened to be at Yaidzu during the three days of the *Bon* or Festival of the Dead ; and I hoped to see the beautiful farewell ceremony of the third and last day. In many parts of Japan, the ghosts are furnished with miniature ships for their voyage, — little models of junks or fishing-craft, each containing offerings of food and water and kindled incense ; also a tiny lantern or lamp, if the ghost-ship be despatched at night. But at Yaidzu lanterns only are set afloat; and I was told that they would be launched after dark. Midnight being the customary hour elsewhere, I supposed that it was the hour of farewell at Yaidzu also ; and I rashly indulged in a nap after supper, expecting to wake up in time for the spectacle. But by ten o'clock, when I went to the beach again, all was over, and everybody had gone home. Over the water I saw something like a long swarm of fire-flies, — the lanterns drifting out to sea in procession ; but they were already too far to be distinguished except as points of colored light. I was much disappointed : I felt that I had lazily missed an opportunity which might never again return, — for these old Bon-customs are dying rapidly. But in another moment it occurred to me that I could very well venture to swim out to the lights. They were moving slowly. I dropped my robe on the beach, and plunged in. The sea was calm,

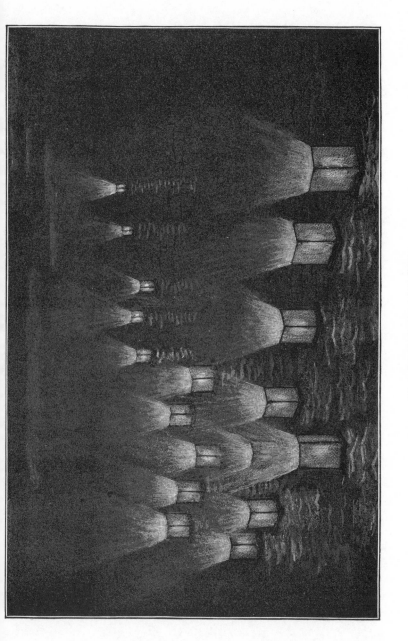

The Lights of the Dead

and beautifully phosphorescent. Every stroke kindled a stream of yellow fire. I swam fast, and overtook the last of the lantern-fleet much sooner than I had hoped. I felt that it would be unkind to interfere with the little embarcations, or to divert them from their silent course : so I contented myself with keeping close to one of them, and studying its details.

The structure was very simple. The bottom was a piece of thick plank, perfectly square, and measuring about ten inches across. Each one of its corners supported a slender stick about sixteen inches high ; and these four uprights, united above by cross-pieces, sustained the paper sides. Upon the point of a long nail, driven up through the centre of the bottom, was fixed a lighted candle. The top was left open. The four sides presented five different colors, — blue, yellow, red, white, and black ; these five colors respectively symbolizing Ether, Wind, Fire, Water, and Earth, — the five Buddhist elements which are metaphysically identified with the Five Buddhas. One of the paper-panes was red, one blue, one yellow; and the right half of the fourth pane was black, while the left half, uncolored, represented white. No *kaimyō* was written upon any of the transparencies. Inside the lantern there was only the flickering candle.

I watched those frail glowing shapes drifting through the night, and ever as they drifted scattering, under impulse of wind and wave, more and more widely apart. Each, with its quiver of color, seemed a life afraid, — trembling on the blind current that was bearing it into the outer blackness. . . . Are not we ourselves as lanterns launched upon a deeper and a dimmer sea, and ever separating further and further one from another as we drift to the inevitable dissolution? Soon the thought-light in each burns itself out: then the poor frames, and all that is left of their once fair colors, must melt forever into the colorless Void. . . .

Even in the moment of this musing I began to doubt whether I was really alone, — to ask myself whether there might not be something more than a mere shuddering of light in the thing that rocked beside me: some presence that haunted the dying flame, and was watching the watcher. A faint cold thrill passed over me, — perhaps some chill uprising from the depths, — perhaps the creeping only of a ghostly fancy. Old super-

stitions of the coast recurred to me, — old vague
warnings of peril in the time of the passage of
Souls. I reflected that were any evil to befall
me out there in the night, — meddling, or seem-
ing to meddle, with the lights of the Dead, — I
should myself furnish the subject of some future
weird legend. . . . I whispered the Buddhist for-
mula of farewell — to the lights, — and made
speed for shore.

As I touched the stones again, I was startled by
seeing two white shadows before me; but a
kindly voice, asking if the water was cold, set me
at ease. It was the voice of my old landlord,
Otokichi the fishseller, who had come to look
for me, accompanied by his wife.

"Only pleasantly cool," I made answer, as I
threw on my robe to go home with them.

"Ah," said the wife, "it is not good to go out
there on the night of the Bon!"

"I did not go far," I replied; — "I only
wanted to look at the lanterns."

"Even a Kappa gets drowned sometimes," [1]
protested Otokichi. "There was a man of this

---

[1] This is a common proverb: — *Kappa mo oboré-shini.*
The Kappa is a water-goblin, haunting rivers especially.

village who swam home a distance of seven *ri*, in bad weather, after his boat had been broken. But he was drowned afterwards."

Seven *ri* means a trifle less than eighteen miles. I asked if any of the young men now in the settlement could do as much.

"Probably some might," the old man replied. "There are many strong swimmers. All swim here, — even the little children. But when fisher-folk swim like that, it is only to save their lives."

"Or to make love," the wife added, — "like the Hashima girl."

"Who ?" queried I.

"A fisherman's daughter," said Otokichi. "She had a lover in Ajiro, several *ri* distant; and she used to swim to him at night, and swim back in the morning. He kept a light burning to guide her. But one dark night the light was neglected — or blown out; and she lost her way, and was drowned. . . . The story is famous in Idzu."

— "So," I said to myself, "in the Far East, it is poor Hero that does the swimming. And what, under such circumstances, would have been the Western estimate of Leander ?"

III

Usually about the time of the Bon, the sea gets rough; and I was not surprised to find next morning that the surf was running high. All day it grew. By the middle of the afternoon, the waves had become wonderful; and I sat on the sea-wall, and watched them until sundown.

It was a long slow rolling, — massive and formidable. Sometimes, just before breaking, a towering swell would crack all its green length with a tinkle as of shivering glass; then would fall and flatten with a peal that shook the wall beneath me. . . . I thought of the great dead Russian general who made his army to storm as a sea, — wave upon wave of steel, — thunder following thunder. . . . There was yet scarcely any wind; but there must have been wild weather elsewhere, — and the breakers were steadily heightening. Their motion fascinated. How indescribably complex such motion is, — yet how eternally new! Who could fully describe even five minutes of it? No mortal ever saw two waves break in exactly the same way.

And probably no mortal ever watched the ocean-roll or heard its thunder without feeling serious. I have noticed that even animals, — horses and cows, — become meditative in the presence of the sea : they stand and stare and listen as if the sight and sound of that immensity made them forget all else in the world.

There is a folk-saying of the coast : — " *The Sea has a soul and hears.*" And the meaning is thus explained : Never speak of your fear when you feel afraid at sea ; — if you say that you are afraid, the waves will suddenly rise higher. . . . Now this imagining seems to me absolutely natural. I must confess that when I am either in the sea, or upon it, I cannot fully persuade myself that it is not alive, — a conscious and a hostile power. Reason, for the time being, avails nothing against this fancy. In order to be able to think of the sea as a mere body of water, I must be upon some height from whence its heaviest billowing appears but a lazy creeping of tiny ripples.

But the primitive fancy may be roused even more strongly in darkness than by daylight. How living seem the smoulderings and the flash-

ings of the tide on nights of phosphorescence!
— how reptilian the subtle shifting of the tints
of its chilly flame! Dive into such a night-sea;
— open your eyes in the black-blue gloom, and
watch the weird gush of lights that follow your
every motion: each luminous point, as seen
through the flood, like the opening and closing
of an eye! At such a moment, one feels indeed
as if enveloped by some monstrous sentiency, —
suspended within some vital substance that feels
and sees and wills alike in every part, — an infinite soft cold Ghost.

IV

Long I lay awake that night, and listened to
the thunder-rolls and crashings of the mighty
tide. Deeper than these distinct shocks of noise,
and all the storming of the nearer waves, was the
bass of the further surf, — a ceaseless abysmal
muttering to which the building trembled, — a
sound that seemed to imagination like the sound
of the trampling of infinite cavalry, the massing
of incalculable artillery, — some rushing, from the
Sunrise, of armies wide as the world.

Then I found myself thinking of the vague terror with which I had listened, when a child, to the voice of the sea; — and I remembered that in after-years, on different coasts in different parts of the world, the sound of surf had always revived the childish emotion. Certainly this emotion was older than I by thousands of thousands of centuries, — the inherited sum of numberless terrors ancestral. But presently there came to me the conviction that fear of the sea alone could represent but one element of the multitudinous awe awakened by its voice. For as I listened to that wild tide of the Suruga coast, I could distinguish nearly every sound of fear known to man: not merely noises of battle tremendous, — of interminable volleying, — of immeasurable charging, — but the roaring of beasts, the crackling and hissing of fire, the rumbling of earthquake, the thunder of ruin, and, above all these, a clamor continual as of shrieks and smothered shoutings, — the Voices that are said to be the voices of the drowned. Awfulness supreme of tumult, — combining all imaginable echoings of fury and destruction and despair!

And to myself I said: — Is it wonderful that the voice of the sea should make us serious?

Consonantly to its multiple utterance must respond all waves of immemorial fear that move in the vaster sea of soul-experience. Deep calleth unto deep. The visible abyss calls to that abyss invisible of elder being whose flood-flow made the ghosts of us.

Wherefore there is surely more than a little truth in the ancient belief that the speech of the dead is the roar of the sea. Truly the fear and the pain of the dead past speak to us in that dim deep awe which the roar of the sea awakens.

But there are sounds that move us much more profoundly than the voice of the sea can do, and in stranger ways, — sounds that also make us serious at times, and very serious, — sounds of music.

Great music is a psychical storm, agitating to unimaginable depth the mystery of the past within us. Or we might say that it is a prodigious incantation, — every different instrument and voice making separate appeal to different billions of prenatal memories. There are tones that call up all ghosts of youth and joy and tenderness; — there are tones that evoke all phantom pain of perished passion; — there are tones that resurrect all dead sensations of majesty and might and glory, — all expired exultations, — all forgotten magnanimities. Well may the influence of music seem inexplicable to the man who idly dreams that his life began less than a hundred years ago! But the mystery lightens for whomsoever learns that the substance of Self is older than the sun. He finds that music is a Necromancy; — he feels that to every ripple of melody, to every billow of harmony, there answers within him, out of the Sea of Death and Birth, some eddying immeasurable of ancient pleasure and pain.

Pleasure and pain: they commingle always in great music; and therefore it is that music can move us more profoundly than the voice of ocean or than any other voice can do. But in music's larger utterance it is ever the sorrow that makes the undertone, — the surf-mutter of the Sea of Soul. . . . Strange to think how vast the sum of joy and woe that must have been experienced before the sense of music could evolve in the brain of man!

Somewhere it is said that human life is the music of the Gods, — that its sobs and laughter, its songs and shrieks and orisons, its outcries of delight and of despair, rise never to the hearing of the Immortals but as a perfect harmony. . . . Wherefore they could not desire to hush the tones of pain : it would spoil their music! The combination, without the agony-tones, would prove a discord unendurable to ears divine.

And in one way we ourselves are as Gods, — since it is only the sum of the pains and the joys of past lives innumerable that makes for us, through memory organic, the ecstasy of music. All the gladness and the grief of dead generations come back to haunt us in countless forms of harmony and of melody. Even so, — a million years after we shall have ceased to view the sun, — will the gladness and the grief of our own lives pass with richer music into other hearts — there to bestir, for one mysterious moment, some deep and exquisite thrilling of voluptuous pain.